Trickster's Ashes

Gwydion Royce

ORACLE OF LOST PATHS BOOKS

Cover Design by Damonza.com

1st edition 2024

Oracle of Lost Paths Books

author@gwydionroyce.com

979-8-9902074-4-8 (eBook)

979-8-9902074-5-5 (Paperback)

Part One

Meg

CHAPTER ONE

I was immediately blinded by the sun as I stepped out onto the beach. Gulls shrieked at me, having had the nerve to just appear in their midst. Anchored wooden ships bobbed gently in the harbor, and farther out, ships with square sails were heading in, riding low in the water, heavy with cargo.

This part of the beach was relatively deserted, most of the activity focused on the bustling midday traffic heading to and from the port. Wagonloads of goods were traveling back and forth, and the shouts of the dock workers carried toward me on the wind.

My eyes traveled the road from the port, back to the city, limestone-washed mudbrick outbuildings bleached by the sun giving way to modest houses on the outskirts of the city proper. The Royal Road wound up and out of sight. My gaze continued upward, and high above on a plateau—I gasped. The palace of Knossos, at its height.

Red-stained cypress columns blazed in the sunlight and the bold pigments splashed across every visible surface gave my eyes plenty to feast on. I wished I could take the time to visit the frescos, but my path was leading me elsewhere. Below ground.

A strong wind tore across the water and caught my skirts, snapping the billowing linen against my legs. I was costumed in a long, flounced skirt with a goldenrod-colored bodice that hugged tightly under my bust, cinched like a girdle. A heavy leather belt was wrapped around my waist and quickly became uncomfortable in the Mediterranean heat.

The style of ancient Minoan Crete would have had me baring my breasts, but I just couldn't bring myself to go adventuring like that. Sometimes things get dangerous and you don't want to have to worry about chaffing your nipples climbing through a tight space, on top of everything else. A valuable life lesson that hadn't steered me wrong yet.

A tendril of my carefully pinned silver hair whipped loose as I made my way down the beach, following the draw of the item I was after. My sandals slipped back and forth in the sand and I was grateful to reach a patch of beach grass. A path was just visible, mostly overgrown and given over to occasional grazing by the looks of it.

When I stepped onto it, I was only a few steps in before I began to feel a heavy weight bearing down on me. There was a strong magick here, and the shadows twisted and morphed in ways the sun should've made impossible.

All sounds of the activity at the port had died away and I was left with the wind in the dry grass and lonely crickets. I pushed through a thick patch of overgrowth and my skin broke out in gooseflesh. I tripped and caught myself on the sandstone face of the plateau.

I could feel etching underneath my fingers, the lines too straight to be natural. I peeled back the high grass and took a peek. Writing had been carved into the rock.

My heritage gave me plenty of built-in knowledge of languages, both living and dead, so once I let my mind go slack and my eyes drift out of focus, my mind translated it into a language I already knew.

"Go back. Death lies ahead. Monsters. Death. Go back." I shivered. If that's not enough to make your butthole clench while alone in the strange wilderness, I don't know what would be.

But I kept walking. I had a job to do, and I wasn't leaving until it was done.

After another minute of walking, I stepped into a small glade, a perfect circle of trees surrounding a bare patch of earth. The heaviness of the magick was the most oppressive here and I resisted clutching my arms around myself.

I stilled. What was that?

The noise came again, a deep booming sound that I also felt underneath my feet, radiating outward from my right. I turned, my eyes going wide as I saw the massive doorway, at least fourteen feet high.

Wait. I scanned the writing etched around the frame. This engraving was harder to read, the language an older version of that used for the graffiti I'd just passed. But I got the gist.

All those legends of the minotaur... I swallowed heavily, double checking that the draw of the item I was seeking was for sure coming from here. I bit back a curse and considered the door. If I was going to complete this task, I would have to risk coming face to face with a myth.

There was no handle anywhere, just a smooth expanse of rock with an intricately carved frame around it. I reached out to trace the edges, searching for a seam, anything, to tell me if it was a real door or just a decoy.

The stone was hot to the touch, and I jerked my hand away. There was no sun breaking through the surrounding trees and the temperature was decent in this little glade. What the hell am I going to find on the other side of this door? Besides the dreaded half man, half bull that ate people.

None of the myths said anything about the beast being some kind of flame-wielding demon, but I guess there's always room for interpretation.

Or maybe it was a portal to hell itself, which, all things considered, wasn't that big of a deal. I had no desire to revisit my old home, but at least I was comfortable there.

I took a deep breath and tapped into the same magick that allowed me to read any language, and spoke the words that I hoped would open the door. The long-dead language slipped off my tongue, twisting it in strange ways. I'd barely finished speaking and the door shuddered, the sound of grating stone setting my teeth on edge as it slid aside to a yawning blackness.

Allowing myself a brief moment of hesitation before I shoved it away, I stepped into the dark. Immediately, the smell of death filled my nostrils, pungent and thick. The sickly sweet stench of rot clung to everything.

It seemed quiet enough, even if the heat was already oppressive and getting worse the farther in I traveled. The ground was so covered in lichen and filth, my footsteps didn't even echo. The limited light spilling in the from the open doorway shone on bronze torch brackets, thick with a heavy patina of age and covered in dust and mold. It had been ages since they were lit, the pitch dried and little more than residue.

"They only light those for the new sacrifices." I murmured. "I should've told them I was coming."

I was met immediately with a choice of three passages and I chose the middle. Minutes passed, then a half hour, then an hour. That booming rumble shook the walls and ground once during my trek, but there was no other sound of life or movement to go with it and it died away, leaving absolute silence in its wake.

The pitted, crumbling stone walls led me in a series of twists and turns, true to the stories of the labyrinth. I'd already tried to transport myself closer to the item now that I had a solid lock on it but there was a block that was preventing my use of magick. It made sense; wouldn't want your sacrifices to escape, or the minotaur to break out, but I was still pissed about it.

The item was so close, I could feel the thrumming in my fingertips as its signature called out to me. One hand was tracing the wall and the other was in front of me, feeling for obstacles. The oppressive darkness began to lighten ever so subtly, and the close stone walls fell away to reveal the center of the maze.

A shaft cut high up in the ceiling was letting weak light trickle into the central chamber, spotlighting the ornate obsidian altar in the middle of the space. Sweat was dripping off my forehead, the girdle cinched around my waist, drenched. The smell was worst here and my focus homed in on a pile of bones and dried fleshy bits.

As I closed in on the altar, I could see the stains of dried blood that coated the surface, mottled brown with age. Claw marks had raked deep gouges in the glassy, black rock.

Just get the damn thing and get out of here, Meg. I tore my eyes away from the grisly scene and spotted a pile of discarded rags with random items strewn among them. I inched closer and realized it was a pile of old clothes, with brooches and jewelry still attached. I dug through the pile, the material disintegrating in my hands, until my fingers grazed a cold, metallic object. I pulled it out and saw that I was holding a chalice, the interior coated with more bloody residue.

A soft snort made me freeze. Slowly, I turned, the light streaming in from overhead catching the glistening of a nose as a creature moved out of the shadows. It was only a few feet away from me and I hadn't even noticed.

The bull-headed beast took a step toward me, the ring through its septum a dull copper, crusted in gunk and embedded in its skin like it had melted into its flesh. There was rage in its eyes, the pupils constricted to tiny pinpricks in its ruddy brown irises.

I was frozen to the spot as the rest of it moved into the light. Eight feet tall, its hide solid black. Its body was human-shaped, its frighteningly muscular shoulders belying a strength that could tear me in half with all the effort of ripping a breadstick. The loincloth around its waist was lifted over its massive erection.

It grabbed me and threw me, sending me sailing into the altar. My ribs landed against the edge, and I cried out in pain as I felt something snap. The minotaur stalked forward and pulled me up by the arm, flipping me onto the altar and pinning me down by the throat.

I punched at its arm, kicking and flailing, anything to get it to loosen its grip. I landed a kick in its gut and it roared, flinging me away from it, into a pile of bones. Dust flew up as the bones pulverized under my weight. There were a few shards that remained solid, and I found a nice, pointy femur.

As the creature bent to grab me, I stabbed up, the bone sinking into its thigh. Its roar was so loud, my attempt at scrambling away was hampered by the clanging in my head. I stumbled and threw my hands out, running them along the wall until I found a break into another path.

I kept moving, quick and quiet, before I realized I'd dropped the chalice.

"Fuck," I hissed. I had to go back.

I crouched against the wall, catching my breath and shaking. I psyched myself up before returning the way I'd come, peeking around the corner just in time to see the beast press its hands against the stone wall. The ground rumbled in the now familiar sensation as a section of the wall moved. The creature disappeared beyond it.

Now or never. I rushed out into the room, snapping up the chalice and sprinting back. The minotaur's arm appeared from the pathway I'd been dashing toward, swiping down at me. I ducked and slid underneath it, my broken rib protesting, running in what I hoped was the right direction. It charged at me, and I barely resisted screaming.

It was big, but I was fast, and I'd soon put distance between us without braining myself headlong into a wall. I dashed around a corner and the minotaur slowed behind me, the clop of its hooves still audible through the layers of filth on the ground.

I held my breath as it neared and moved past. Waiting was agony. Every time it stopped, I expected it to come bursting through the wall or move another panel. The steps receded and I heard deep snuffling noises as it tried to sniff me out.

Finally, everything was silent. I thought I knew the general direction of the exit. Ingrained sense of time and space is one of the perks of being me. The ability for time travel itself isn't bad, but there are a whole lot of strings attached. And the whole mess of what I was expected to do with it—

The minotaur roared in frustration, and I flattened myself against the wall. He sounded far away but there was a long run to the exit, and he had home court advantage.

Maybe the other panels moved too. I pressed my hands against the stone and pushed. Not this one. I tried the next and the next. No luck.

The next one I tried moved a tiny fraction. I pushed, firmly but slowly, trying to make as little noise as possible. It rumbled, but not nearly with the same ferocity as before. I'd moved it enough to squeeze through and followed the same procedure in the next corridor.

Intermittent pauses to listen still put the minotaur a ways from me. I could actually see the light starting to seep in from the open doorway ahead, just a subtle brightening. I abandoned the search for the moveable panels and started to wind my way through the maze again.

A breeze tickled my skin.

The minotaur roared right behind me and charged. I shrieked and bolted for the exit, taking a turn too sharply and clipping my shoulder on the edge. I stumbled into a wall and banged my head against the stone, the stars in my eyes slowing me down to a stumbling pace.

The ground shook as the beast moved a panel. The light was so bright, the air was fresh and cool as it coursed down the passage. I came to a T-junction and light was streaming from both sides so they should both lead me where I wanted to go. I chose the passage on the right and ran, my head clear again.

The minotaur stepped directly into my path but I didn't slow down. As I neared, its bull snout twisted in a pointy-toothed grin, a vision I was sure was going to revisit me in my nightmares, and reached its arms out for me. I dropped and slid, making sure to grip the chalice tightly. The lichen added momentum, and I picked up speed as I shot right through its wide-legged stance and popped up on the other side, continuing my sprint. I turned one last corner and could have cried as the doorway was revealed. The minotaur was right on my heels.

As I neared the exit, I shouted at the door to "Close, close, close!"

The stone doorway shuddered and began to slide. I squeezed through with just enough space and felt the dappled sunlight on my face when the minotaur's clawed hand fisted in my bodice and jerked me back. The door jammed on its arm and it bellowed, forcing its other arm through and pushing the massive door back open.

I slammed my forearm into the beast's, trying to break its hold, but it didn't do any good. It stepped out of its labyrinth and was momentarily dazed when a shaft of sunlight hit its eyes. I took my chance.

I tapped the time stream and hurled us both through, heading for the lodge and the backup that would be waiting there.

We shifted back into the current timeline in a small storage room. The minotaur was staring, frozen to the spot, and I was able to break his hold, slipping out the door and slamming it behind me and sliding the bolt home. All the doors down here were reinforced with steel. You never know when things are going to get crazy and this wouldn't be the first time I'd brought back a clinger.

The minotaur howled and battered its fists against the door. The sibling duo, Risha and Ursal, trundled down the stairs at the noise.

"What happened?" asked Ursal.

I grinned sheepishly. "Surprise."

Chapter Two

A quick change of clothes and a shower were in order. Getting the barnyard stench off me was a chore, and I didn't have much hope that we could salvage the costume I'd worn. I'd kept it far away from the other outfits in my extensive wardrobe of period clothing from all over the world, just in case the smell tried to cling to the others. Having an outfit ready to go that would blend into any time period was a must for the frequent traveler.

The drive home was a nice refresh. The lodge was up in the mountains and served as our base of operations to keep our activity concealed. We weren't doing anything untoward, but the High Council that ruled all matters involving the Strangefells and its realms didn't know anything about what we were up to. It was important to keep it that way.

The lodge was also a staging ground for operations as well as a research and development lab that Risha used to investigate the objects, the links, I'd brought back over the years. She and her twin brother, Ursal, had joined us at the outset.

The two were perfectly capable of dealing with the minotaur on their own. They were our oldest friends and allies, and they were nephilim, beings of superior size and strength. Compared to my slight, barely five-foot-five frame, they were a much better match for that thing.

All I wanted to do was go home and snuggle up with my better half. Maybe take a nice, relaxing bath later. I cranked up the tunes and hit the gas.

"Remind me to never mess with a minotaur again."

Bel whirled around from where he'd been standing, startled. He hadn't heard me come in. The alarm in his dark-brown eyes eased, and his sharp features softened with a grin. He opened his arms and welcomed me in, and I gladly enveloped myself in his warmth. A cascade of black hair fell around me as I breathed him in, the stresses of my journey fading away.

"I barely escaped it. I couldn't tell if it wanted to eat me or fuck me."

"Maybe both." Bel moved us over to the couch and I sank into it with a sigh. I grabbed a blanket and wrapped myself up.

"Wine? Something stronger?" he asked, smoothing some flyaway hairs down.

"Wine's good."

I stretched, reclining, and sank into the deep cushions. I kept myself moving, trying to work the knots out of my muscles and to keep myself awake so I could at least give him the mission debrief.

Bel came back with two glasses of red wine, and I took a sip, letting the taste flow over my tongue and wash away the lingering dirt and all-around unpleasant experiences I'd returned from.

The couch indented as Bel's comforting weight settled next to me and my body instinctively moved toward him. His arm wrapped around my shoulders as I rested my head on him and sipped my wine, taking a moment to listen to his heartbeat and the breath going in and out of his lungs. I breathed in his scent again.

"Is that the cologne I got you for our anniversary?"

"Mm-hmm." His fingers dragged up my side and back down in a slow, calming motion. "So do you want to talk about it?"

"I'm assuming Ursal already called you about the bull in the storage closet?" I tried to laugh at my own joke, but it just turned into an exhausted wheeze.

"He did. They got it under control and are keeping it detained until we can figure out where to send it."

I sighed and rolled my shoulders again. Bel pulled away and motioned for me to lean forward. Nimble fingers moved my hair out of the way and started a glorious massage. My eyes drifted closed and I enjoyed the sensations before continuing with the story. "The item was a chalice, and I had to wander through a sealed labyrinth to get to it."

"What time period?" The rumble in his chest made me vibrate, physically and mentally. I was always so damn turned on when I came back from treasure hunting.

Focus. "Crete, peak Minoan civilization."

Bel chuckled. "I didn't witness much of them myself, but what I did see was impressive. Not until the Greeks took on Persia did I see such naval prowess again. Such a shame it crumbled." He thought for a moment. "So the myths were real, then."

I nodded. "Unfortunately. But the palace was breathtaking." I let the vista sweep through my memory again, wanting to cement every detail forever. Sure, I could go back whenever I wanted, but the first time you witness something like that is always the best.

Bel's fingers traced a light trail on my arm, sending delicious shivers up my spine. I sipped my wine and refocused on the story, taking him with me down the creepy, overgrown path.

"I half expected some kind of ancient Jason Voorhees to come jumping out of the scrub with a hockey mask on."

Another squeeze. "I'm sorry you have to go on these missions alone. I wish I could go with you."

"To help fight monsters or to see the sights for yourself?" I teased.

His eyes crinkled at the corners. "I will fight any monster you need me to. As long as I get to explore after."

"Uh-huh." I ran my fingers across his stubble, tone turning serious. "I know you would, and we both know you can't. Not unless the stakes are a lot lower." The amount of power it would take to transport us both would leave me too drained if we had to travel again in a hurry.

The more power someone possessed, the harder it was for me to transport them with me. I likened it to checked baggage versus carry on. Someone like Bel, an ancient and supreme power among the Ætherim, had a high "spiritual density," which made him harder to move through time. It was possible, but there would be an extra fee involved.

Heat lanced to my core as his fingers started brushing the top of my breast. I smiled at him. "Do you want to just skip the debrief and head upstairs?"

Bel looked up, surprised, and moved his hand back to my shoulder. "Sorry. Continue." A wicked grin. "I'll make it up to you after."

I shook my head but carried on with the story. "So of course I kept walking toward danger, death, and monsters." The butterflies fluttered in my stomach again as I recalled it. "The doors had to have been twice as tall as you, which is never a good start."

Bel stretched his almost seven-foot frame in response. "How'd you break through?"

I shrugged. "Asked nicely for it to open."

He shifted, and I looked up to meet his questioning gaze. I smiled and took a large gulp of wine. "Granted, I was speaking an ancient Minoan dialect. I doubt it would have understood American English."

Bel's chest jumped as he snorted and the burst of breath ruffled my hair. A beeping sound from the kitchen pierced the calm and Bel eased me aside before hurrying to the kitchen.

"Did you make snacks?" I asked, hopefully. My stomach growled on cue.

"Sure did." His voice was muffled and then I heard the oven door snap shut. "I warmed up those leftover meat pies from Yvonne."

"Perfect." Mouth already watering, my eyes landed on the plate of food Bel carried back into the living room. I risked the burned fingertips and grabbed one off the plate, taking a big bite.

"Hot." I chewed through the pain, tears in my eyes, and swallowed... before taking another bite. Bel just watched me eat and shook his head. He didn't bother to wonder why I did weird things anymore.

Once I'd polished off a meat pie, the story was ready to continue. "Anyway. The door opened to a black hole."

His voice was flat. "And you stepped through it."

"Of course I did. I eat scorching hot food and step into any dark abyss I find. I have no concern for my personal safety." Finishing the wine in my glass, Bel poured me a fresh one.

With a surreptitious gliding of my hand, I cupped Bel's crotch while I swirled the wine in my glass. His breath hitched and his hand moved low on my waist while I played coy.

I stared at the red liquid in my glass. "I thought that was it. When the beast had me in its grip. I was so disoriented from the darkness, and the noise and getting thrown. Then I had to find my way back out with it chasing me down."

"My gods." Bel kissed the top of my head. "I'm so sorry I couldn't be there to help you."

His sincerity warmed my heart, and I nuzzled into him. He tilted my face up and kissed my lips before reluctantly drawing away. "Why don't I run you a bath and you can have a soak? I'll bring up wine and more snacks and you can relax for a bit."

"That sounds nice. I'll take you up on that."

A glint in his eye made my stomach flutter, and then he said the words I'd been wanting to hear since I got back. "I can join you if you'd like."

"Speaker of the magick words. My hero." I pretended to swoon and Bel headed upstairs, an anticipatory chuckle rumbling in his chest.

The night was warm and a pleasant breeze was coming in through the open window as I curled up next to Bel. The night had been a blur of relief-seeking sex that always satisfied in the moment, but it never lasted long. I'd always had a healthy libido but ever since I started to time travel on the regular, my cravings had gotten worse.

Bel moaned in his sleep and I reached up to stroke his cheek. His eyes opened a crack, and he focused on me. "Did I wake you?" he asked.

"No." I rested my chin on his chest and smiled at him creepily. "I've been watching you sleep."

He made a strangled noise as he pulled a face.

I laughed and rolled onto my back, pulling myself to sitting. Bel did the same, kissing my shoulder. "I would've thought you'd be exhausted enough to sleep for a couple of days straight after tonight."

I shrugged. "My mind won't slow down. All I can think about is getting this task over with." I tucked my knees into my chest and wrapped my arms around them, resting my head on my legs as I looked at Bel with a tired smile. "And I'm still worked up. I don't suppose you can go another few rounds."

"Still?" Bel shook his head. "It's got to be related to the Six. The closer you get to finding them and the more you're exposed to the residual energy the other links to the Titans possess, it must manifest in you being…"

"Horny as fuck?"

Bel laughed. "Once this is over and we've secured all remaining ties to the Titans, the urges might lessen. And you can be proud of the fact that you've succeeded in keeping those beasts locked away forever." He stroked my chin "That should give you a good night's sleep right there."

I stretched and pulled the covers up. "There shouldn't be that many links left now. The Desma are the ones I need to focus on, but I can't get a lock on them. I need to rethink my search tactics. I always block out my own signature so it doesn't interfere, but maybe I need to do the opposite."

It would stand to reason that our signatures would be similar. I was created by the Titans. The Desma, or the Six, were an elusive group of people that had been right hands to the Titans at the height of their power. They became so interconnected, they probably would have absorbed the Titans signature into themselves.

That magickal signature is what I use when I'm trying to locate the links. It's a residue, a homing beacon that you can't turn off. If you know what to look for, you can find someone or something anywhere, across time and space.

The Desma were the biggest threat to the success of our venture. As long as they were wandering through time somewhere, the Titans would have a connection to this world. And through that connection, those monsters could exercise a plan for escape, or worse. Kronos and the rest weren't the types that would just sail off quietly into the sunset with their newfound freedom.

Bel's voice took on a hard edge. "We've already talked about that. It could make you vulnerable to their influence, open you up to them turning the tables on you. They may not even know you exist. Connecting to them directly will not only ruin the element of surprise but possibly put you in danger. You can't give them that power over you." He settled back down. "Give yourself some grace. You'll figure it out. I'm sure there are many fail-safes against finding them the Titans put in place that we haven't even discovered yet. We'll get through it. Together."

The anger and resentment flared up as it always did when I thought about my "family" and everything they'd done. My fingernails bit into my skin and I winced. "How can I hate people I've never met this much?"

Just like that, I started to spiral, all my baggage heaping on top of me when I allowed myself even a small bit of retrospection.

"Baby, you can't do this to yourself."

When I showed no sign of coming out of my fetal position, he settled for stroking my hair. "You were created as a weapon for them to use. To break their chains and go back to wreaking havoc on this world. They never saw you as a person."

"Because I'm not a person. I'm a construct." The words dripped from my mouth like poison. "It was purely accidental that I developed a mind of my own. The gave their golem too much free will."

His hand stilled briefly before continuing its pattern. "I don't see you that way. Nobody that knows you would either. No matter your origins, you are *you*. And I love you for exactly that."

"That doesn't make it less true. I'm energy and will, formed into flesh and blood with ancient magick and a sprinkle of cosmic dust for flavor."

"Megiste."

I looked up at the use of my full name. The name my "father," Kronos, gave me before sending me up the circles of hell to be raised by creatures only a bit less monstrous than the Titans themselves.

"Should we call this operation off for a while? The Desma will be waiting when you're ready to take up the task again, but I can't just sit by and watch the memories tear you apart."

I smiled and rested my forehead against his. "Thank you. But I can't stop now. I'm just feeling sorry for myself." I snuggled back under the covers, pulling Bel down with me. We got comfortable, and I closed my eyes, willing my insomnia away. "I'll be fine in the morning."

Chapter Three

Amazingly, it worked. I woke to bright sunlight streaming through the blinds and an early afternoon buzz of noise. There was a soft knock, and I rolled over to see Bel padding across the thick carpet with two cups of coffee in hand. He sat, not spilling a drop from mugs full to the brim, and waited for me to sit up and hold out eager hands for the cup of morning salvation.

"Feeling any better?" he asked, peering closely at me, looking for lies.

I nodded, mouth full of hot coffee. I swallowed with a heavy gulp. "Very much. Told you I'd be fine."

"Have any weird dreams?" He pretended to be nonchalant, one eyebrow peaked as he sipped his own coffee, not looking at me.

I tilted my head, considering. "Now you mention it, yeah. As far as I can remember they were pretty typical, just more vivid than usual. Why?"

"You were moving quite a bit and murmuring something in your sleep." He hummed. "Almost sounded like a conversation."

I sat back farther into my pillows, an odd chill and foreboding creeping in. "Weird. I don't remember anything specific."

"It didn't seem like you were troubled. I just don't remember you ever doing something like that before."

I frowned. "Not that anyone's ever told me anyway."

Bel set his coffee mug down with a dull *thunk* on the bedside table and turned to me. "You should look for another target. Today."

Hot coffee almost spewed from my mouth as I choked. "What? What about all that you said last night? About taking some time off?"

Earnestness creased his face. "And you said there was no need."

"But I also take at least a couple weeks between. Why the rush?"

Bel sat back and worked at his neck muscles with an absent hand. "I can't really explain it. I know the clock is ticking. The sooner we get this done, the better."

He slid out of bed and took his coffee mug with him. "I've got some breakfast going, join me when you're ready. I'll be heading to the lodge later."

Nodding, I focused on my coffee. Whatever urgency he was feeling couldn't be related to the Titans. I would know.

Bel had been on the front lines with the other Æther-im during the Titan wars, witnessed the destruction they'd wrought firsthand. He was the one person in my life that understood the full significance of what we were trying to accomplish. But even so, I had an inside track he just didn't have access to. I may not have direct contact with them, but I can always tell when there's a glut of Titanic energy getting ready to cause trouble.

Maybe heading back to the lodge wasn't such a bad idea. At the very least, I could talk it over with Risha and get her take. Some of the twins' ancestors had fought alongside Bel and they'd heard the stories. I valued her opinion. Even though they didn't have as much at stake—their entire identity wasn't on the line—they had my best interests at heart.

I sighed. I'd long since lost count of how many years I'd been hunting down links to the Titans and how many places I'd gone to find them.

The links took many forms. There were objects, like the chalice. They usually only had passing connection to the Titans and were much easier to get a lock on and collect. When they weren't in the middle of a labyrinth, that is.

There had also been a few living people, mostly sorcerers. They'd never had direct contact with the Titans, but were devoted to their worship, keeping their memory, and therefore their energy, alive.

There were even occasionally animals, familiars of magi I'd apprehended who had been the high priests or priestesses of a Titan's mystery cult.

And of course there were the Desma, the six currently nameless and faceless Strangers that were top of the most wanted list.

When you're dealing with beings as powerful as the Titans, there's no knowing how they could manipulate any and all connections they can latch onto, even sealed away in Tartarus. The best way to ensure all ties are cut is to make sure every link is destroyed or imprisoned. With no connection to the outside world anymore, the Titans will be entirely helpless to act.

Clearly, I'm a bit of a speed bump in that theory, but when Bel saved me from the gilded cage I'd been raised in almost three decades ago, he'd promised to protect me. He knew of a way to sever all my ties to the Titans but it was imperative that I find the links and the Desma first.

When Kronos created me, I looked like a human baby. The Titans powers had been suppressed, but there's only so much you can do to tie down beings descended from creatures that were forged from the primordial soup of the universe.

Kronos himself sent me to the upper reaches of the underworld to be raised by the rare Ætherim that were on their side. With the promise that those Ætherim would gain great power when the Titans were free, of course. They weren't acting out of the good will of their own hearts.

When the Ancients broke free of their cages last year and tore up a city in Michigan, Bel and I knew we had to do something. One Ancient had almost destroyed an entire city in a single night. And now that the entire world was aware of the existence of the Strangefells, magick was running far too freely in the human world again. The darkness was peeling back, and creatures of all sorts were waking up. The Ancients were the worst of them, sure. But if Titans and elder Ætherim started to stomp around again, there would be worse consequences than a busted-up city.

And with the world watching our community closely, there wasn't a lot of room for error. A small but dedicated team working outside official channels to ensure the Titans would never breathe free air again sounded like the best option. I certainly didn't want the High Council or their enforcers on our asses, but I'd take my chances.

Bel had warm pastries waiting when I came downstairs, empty coffee mug in hand. He waited until I'd taken a few bites before sitting across from me and leaning forward on his elbows.

"Give any more thought to what I asked?"

"I'm not entirely sure I'm comfortable with it. I haven't sensed anything changing. This last trip already sent me for a bit of a loop. I'd like at least a few more days before diving back in."

A small hiss escaped Bel's throat, and I looked up just in time to see a flash of anger cross his face. He was quick to hide it behind a strained smile. "Of course. You know your limits. If you're sure that's what you need, I'll respect it."

"You've kind of got me reeling with this sudden attitude shift. What's going on?" I hated disappointing him, but I also didn't want to overexert myself. The side effects had been getting more and more extreme with each jump through time.

Bel turned away and looked out the window, troubled.

I nibbled at a pastry. "Let's just go to the lodge and catch up with the twins. We can talk about it more on the way," I offered. Bel nodded curtly but his shoulders relaxed a touch. I reached over and took his hand. "Is there something you're not telling me?"

He shook his head. "I really can't be sure."

"Did something happen last night?"

His fingers traced the edge of his breakfast plate. "I told you I thought you were having a conversation in your dream?"

My brows knit, and I nodded.

"I swear I heard the words 'you don't control me.'"

My heart thudded painfully, and my breath hitched. "Wait. Do you think—"

"Not for certain. But what if all this travel and handling of the links is making your connection to the Titans stronger? We've been able to block them out so far, but if that connection strengthens—"

"So we rework the blocks. Figure out something stronger."

"That'll only be a patch, nothing permanent. If this is happening, speed is our only option."

My hands became far more interesting all of a sudden. I pushed my chair back in a rush, and it caught on the tile. I pitched backward, catching myself right before I hit the counter. Bel moved to get up and help me, but I waved him off as I stood.

My hands shook as they found the coffee pot and poured a fresh cup. I clasped my fingers around it tight, seeking the warmth that had leeched out of my body.

Bel seemed to realize the weight of his words. "Hey, don't do that. Don't panic before we know for sure."

I sneered. "I think I'm allowed to feel a little anxious, don't you?"

He held up his hands in surrender. "You absolutely are." He crossed the kitchen and pulled me into a hug. "Go get ready. Once we're at the lodge I think we'll both feel better about a lot of things."

Chapter Three

The trip was silent, the interior of Bel's latest high-end car whisper quiet. He did like the finer things in life, offering several times to buy me whatever kind of vehicle I'd like. He found it adorable that I chose a modest sedan and had been driving the same one for years.

Truth was, I would have been happy with a bicycle or a pogo stick. Nice things are no replacement for a family, and I got my fill of the high life while trapped in the underworld.

The summer was in full swing, and the convertible top was down as we drove through the mountains. The lodge was about an hour away from our house in the foothills of Mount Ascutney, through miles of winding roads before our private drive hidden in the trees led to a cozy cabin that had been a hunting lodge before Bel bought it. Fitting, all things considered.

The drive was paved with a thin layer of asphalt that was already breaking apart after one harsh Vermont winter. I'd warned Bel not to cheap out on the construction, but there were still some aspects of the human world that he didn't catch on to easily; the impermanence of asphalt being one.

Several mods and a few underground chambers later, and it was ready for hosting operations. Shadow obscured the clearing as a cloud rolled over the sun, adding a momentary sense of doom to the place that was already one step away from a horror movie set. But it kept people away, so I guess I could deal with the momentary flashes of anxiety thinking that a twisted creature would reach from behind a tree and grab me.

As we got out of the car, Ursal stepped onto the front porch, the nephilim's head almost brushing the top of the doorframe—which we'd had custom-built to accommodate his height. The only good thing about the outing of the Strangefells: Ursal could go out in public without people asking if the circus was in town.

He hailed us with a smile. Bel trailed behind me as I joined him on the porch.

"Everything alright?" asked Ursal, pulling me into a side hug.

Damn, I thought I'd nailed my "brave face." My shoulders slumped. "Is it that obvious?"

Ursal stroked his trimmed blond beard and shrugged, a small smile on his face. "It was just a question. You assumed I thought you were troubled."

"Ugh. Don't start with your mind games, mutant."

He chuckled. Anybody else would've gotten their arms ripped off for pointing out his troubled heritage. Humans and angels—fallen or no—had certainly made some interesting offspring.

Ursal flung his arm around my shoulders and steered me inside. "So what was it this time? Dreams? Cravings?"

"Both," I grumbled. "It's just getting worse." I motioned helplessly at Bel, who was tapping away on his phone, not hearing a word of what I was saying. "And Bel thinks that I might have been doing more than dreaming last night. Possibly visiting with the Titans."

The nephilim's face turned stern in a flash. "What? But you don't remember it?"

Bel's phone clicked off, and I turned as he slid it back into his pocket. "There are many items on the agenda for today." He looked at his watch. "Is Risha here yet?"

Ursal nodded toward the back of the cabin, where the stairs would take us down to the subterranean chambers and our R & D department. "She's been working on the chalice. I don't think she even went home last night." I could hear his concern for his twin sister's single-minded dedication to a job. Once Risha had her hands on a new project, she ate, slept, and breathed it until it was finished.

"So what's the word on the chalice?" I asked.

Ursal hesitated. "It's a definite maybe."

I blanched and he continued driving the stake into my heart. "The link is weak, most likely used in a ritual dedicated to the Titans at some point, but they didn't have direct contact with it."

"Dammit." My stomach sank. "That makes the past three objects I've recovered of little significance. I wasted all that effort for nothing."

"Maybe not nothing." Ursal's voice echoed in the tight stairwell as we reached the bottom and emptied into the sprawling underground chamber. "I think you're just casting too broad a net, so you're finding anything and everything that's ever made contact with a Titan in one way or another."

"And maybe you're avoiding the big-ticket targets?" asked Bel with a raised eyebrow. "Aiming for the stuff that appears less menacing?"

When I opened my mouth to argue, he cut me off. "I don't blame you. The first time you went after a living target he almost killed you. It's a big risk, especially if we're talking about the elite."

I let that sit for a beat. "But one you still want me to take."

"Don't you?" Bel was already halfway across the room to check in on Risha's progress.

Ursal sidled up next to me and bumped me gently with his elbow. "Don't let him get to you. That's how he hides how worried he is about you. He's just got a lousy way of showing it."

I crossed my arms in front of my chest. "Yeah, well, he does have a point."

Ursal grinned. He knew how hard it was for me to say that. "We shouldn't be talking about this until we figure out what the deal is with your side effects ratcheting up."

Bel raised his voice across the chamber, his booming baritone echoing in the concrete box of the basement. I plugged my ears and gave him a pointed look. With a sheepish grin, he started again. "I already told her we needed to pick up the pace. That's the only option. Stronger blocks won't work. Not for long. And it might end up impeding her ability to home in on the links and the Desma." He turned to Risha. "Don't you agree?"

Risha looked around, her eyes huge behind a ridiculous pair of magnifying goggles. "Agree with what?" She blinked and started as the conversation registered in her brain. "Oh, right." She waved dismissively and went back to her work. "It's a fair point. Time is of the essence."

"Did you just make a joke?" I asked, shocked.

Risha ignored me. Bel was leaning over her shoulder, watching her work and talking in quiet murmurs. Ursal was busying himself going through the small library. That left me to wander until they decided what course of action they wanted to take. At the risk of insulting myself, I realized they were the brains, and I was the brawn.

I headed toward the "trophy" room to revisit my recent failures. Maybe that would give me the kick in the ass I needed to get it right next time.

The almost five dozen items were cataloged and displayed on shelves in meticulous fashion, information about their origin neatly printed on little cards just like a museum.

The most recent additions were at the far right of the middle shelf. A book that had been used by a dabbler in the occult who summoned the spirit of a former magus that had served the Titans. A knife that had been used in a ritual sacrifice of a goat by a mystery cult that worshipped those monsters a thousand years after the Titans were locked away. They'd also cleared space for my latest fuck up, the chalice.

My cheeks burned with the embarrassment of my failures. I needed to redeem myself on the next one, find a Desma.

Bel had told me stories about the battles, entire cities wiped out in an afternoon, the Titans fully manifest in their true size and form as they savaged the land and destroyed the people. Strangers of all sorts filled the ranks of their armies and the rare Ætherim that took the Titans' side.

Clouds of smoke often hung heavy for days in the war path, so impenetrable it was like they'd brought Tartarus with them. Bel would so vividly relive the Titans' monstrous armies appearing out of the smoke, eyes blazing, dripping with blood and ichor. It was enough to give me nightmares. That's why I was doing this. That's why this work had to continue.

Even if I hadn't already hated them for damning me to a life where I was never meant to have free will or a mind of my own, the carnage they'd reap if they escaped... I couldn't imagine the kind of wrath that would have been festering for millennia.

Realization dawned that I'd wandered to the door to the lower levels, where any living links began their captivity with us. And where the Desma would spend the rest of their days. I'd never seen those rooms with my own eyes. Bel knew it would remind me too much of the circumstances of my childhood.

The prisoners were kept well enough, a gilded cage just like mine had been. According to Bel there was a small chamber below where they would arrive after I sent them through and then after they were put into the system by Risha, and she had the answers she needed, they'd be off to a pocket dimension where their prison had been created.

They'd never be free, but they wouldn't be a threat any longer. They made their choices when they joined the side of tyrants. I was just coming to collect on their debts.

My hands brushed the doorknob. It wouldn't hurt to take a peek. I'd always been curious about—

"Meg!"

I whirled around at Bel's sharp call. Eyes wide and mouth parted, he had frozen mid step, staring at my hand on the doorknob. When I moved away from the door, he melted back into the easy stance and slow smile, like he hadn't been about ready to tackle me.

"What's wrong?" I asked.

"Are you feeling up to a search?" He nodded his head back toward the main room. "Come on." He walked away without checking to see if I would follow.

Confusion weighed heavily on me as I joined the rest of the team, stomach churning uneasily. I wiped my palms on my shorts as I stepped into the mini-huddle they had going.

"I think it will be more effective if you perform the search within a protective circle this time," said Risha. She'd already sketched out a circle in chalk on the concrete floor and filled it in with symbols and shapes that I recognized but didn't know what they meant.

"Because that will amplify my ability to home in on the Desma or because it will shield me from the Titans?"

Risha smiled apologetically. "I'm hoping for the latter. It's going to be up to you to find a way to pinpoint the Six."

"Are you ready?" Bel searched my face, taking my elbows in his hands. "It's okay if you're not, we can leave it for a couple of days. But—"

I held up my hand. "It's fine. I understand the need for it. I'll do it."

A relieved smile lit up Bel's face and my heart melted. Ultimately, I'd do anything this man asked of me. He'd sacrificed so much to save me, but it wasn't just the debt I owed him; I genuinely loved him.

They brought down some pillows and a blanket so I could nestle in the middle of the circle. I preferred a semi-reclined position so I wouldn't fall asleep, but still felt like I was heavy and cradled as I sank into the trance.

Bel and the twins disappeared upstairs to give me space and quiet. One of them hit the lights on the way up and the room was cast into eerie shadows as the recessed accent lighting was the only glow that remained.

I breathed deep, closing my eyes. I sank farther and farther down until I felt heavy and sluggish, like a weighted blanket was draped over me. After a while, I felt a new sensation, like my body was floating. My soul was free and ready to travel.

Chapter Four

Traveling through time itself was easy. The swirling currents pushed against me with pressure, like walking through a deep river with waders on, but against my skin it always felt soft and warm, like steam. Colors and light blurred around me and within seconds I was in another time and place. Now the hard part. Figuring out what I was after.

As I stood in the purgatory between worlds, a vast, gray void of fog and shadow, I began to filter through the various signatures I was already familiar with as having a connection to the Titans. What was I missing that would lead me to the Six?

The only reason I even knew about them was because of Bel's stories. He'd figured out their importance when they disappeared off the face of the earth after the Titans fell. No way would Kronos's most loyal servants abandon the fight unless they'd been made to leave or hidden away. If I could find them, that could very well be the death blow to the Titans' plans.

There was one thing I'd never dared to try, afraid of what it might lead to. Bel had laid out all the risks plainly, warning me away. But the gods only knew how much time we'd have left before the Titans began to ramp up their efforts. It was now or never.

I tuned in to my own magickal signature, my unique essence, and let it seep into every bit of my awareness. Then I cast it out, letting it fly into the void, seeking similar energies. I watched the glittering silver trails flow away from me, bright in the dim gray light, programmed with their assignment of what to find. And then I waited.

It could have been ten minutes or ten hours, but eventually there was a tug on one of the lines. I sharpened my focus on the target and an orb appeared, pulsating in response to my call.

My heart sped up, and my fingers traced the thin cord, reeling it in with a gentle touch. With each tug I received more information from whatever was on the other end. The time period was the easiest. Medieval Germany, during the reign of Charlemagne. A figure began to form next. A large man, broad shouldered with scars on his face, hands battered from a life of hard work. The setting filled out around him, and I could see stone walls, archways, and a courtyard filled with bright, early morning light.

The man turned and smiled as a small group of people bustled by, nodding and laughing at something one of them said. A few ladies in fine dresses entered the courtyard arm in arm, to enjoy the gardens. The elder woman noticed the man and glared at him, her grimace of disgust making it clear that she wasn't happy a commoner was invading their space. The man gathered his things and hurried out of sight.

He moved to another part of the castle where there were no courtiers to bother him and continued his work, patching masonry and repairing damage that looked like it had been caused by fire.

Arthur. His name popped into my head. Could this be one of the elite? He didn't quite... fit, in the picture that was forming. His carriage was more regal than a tradesperson, a man that was used to being important and commanding a room instead of running from the glares of nobles. Power exuded from him, an intimidating force. The easy, genuine smile is what threw me off.

Not what I would expect from a man that held high esteem with monsters. Maybe the higher up they were, the better they were at deceit. He was powerful, but for all I knew his connection was through a girlfriend that got him involved in a mystery cult and the only reason I found him was because I was trying something new. There were still plenty of things I didn't understand about my own magick.

I'd have to make damn sure that he was the man I was after before bringing back another dud. There wouldn't be ridicule per se, but I'd be letting Bel and the twins down, nonetheless. I'd be letting myself down.

Arthur stilled and looked around, curious. Then his eyes fastened on mine. I reeled back, pulling away from him, all the way out of the void and back into my body. My soul thudded back into place almost painfully, and my head protested, flaring with a raging headache that blazed across my forehead.

What the fuck? Did he see me? Or did he feel eyes on him and just happened to look in my direction?

I waited for my pulse to slow and the pounding in my head to ebb before I reluctantly left my nest of pillows and blankets and got to my feet. Every step up the stairs to the main lodge felt like I was carrying a hundred extra pounds on my back.

Everyone was sitting in the kitchen, conversing around the island in hushed voices. They looked up as I entered.

"What's wrong?" Bel was at my side in a flash, pressing a sports drink into my hands. Light fingers smoothed the hair from my forehead. "Are you okay?"

"Yeah. Things got weird, is all."

Risha sounded alarmed. "How weird?"

I opened my mouth to tell them about the Desma but decided better of it. No matter how shaken I was, I didn't want to risk being wrong. And I definitely didn't want to get their hopes up that I'd found an elite.

My mouth snapped shut and I forced a grin on my face. "The usual hunt got a bit intense. There's a promising lead, but I won't know for sure until I see it up close."

"Living or an object?" asked Ursal.

I shrugged. "Not sure yet, but it feels strong." From the corner of my eye, I could see Bel frown.

The tightness in his voice matched the judgment in his gaze. "Are you feeling up to going after it?"

A slug of the sports drink sent fruit-punch-flavored electrolytes flooding into my system. I held up my finger while I downed the rest of the bottle in a few long pulls.

With a satisfied sigh, I nodded, all while trying to ignore the growing sense of foreboding. "Let's do it."

The main thing I learned in all my traveling between worlds and time periods, was that the simplest thing I could do to keep myself safe was to dress appropriately. I'd gathered quite the costume collection over the years as I prepared to fit in with whatever era I needed to explore.

If I was really in a pinch, I would settle for stealing garments, but since most people in long-ago eras only owned a few sets of clothing in a lifetime, I hated doing it.

I had the gift of language, given from Mnemosyne more than likely, so that was never a problem. Adapting to the spoken and written languages of the time and place was a subconscious endeavor, coming naturally without thought. One of the only good things being a Titans' construct had added to my life.

Now, as I stepped through the archway of the city gates, I was as prepared as I could be for the task at hand. I'd told Bel this one could take longer. Guilt gnawed at me for skirting the truth about why, but I had to be sure. Already something about this mission didn't feel right. Due diligence was the only way I was getting answers, and that meant going undercover and sleuthing it out.

I'd never done it this way before, preferring to be in and out as quick as possible to avoid unnecessary clashes. Understanding the language and looking the part was one thing, and cultural differences were decently easy to pick up on, but there were still small things. Societal constructs that were impossible to understand from a modern perspective, or colloquialisms that didn't make it into the cosmic lexicon that I was drawing from. Little mistakes added up to many raised eyebrows and could get me in trouble.

And the distant past was far less hesitant to burn the witch.

The day was warm, and I was already sweating in my layers of simple linen clothing, hair tucked into a tight-fitting cap. While playing the part of a noble might have been fun, nobody looks twice at the peasant girl. The only thing not authentic was my shoes, which were thick leather, but they were mostly hidden under long skirts.

I wasn't sure what my plan was. Waltzing into the castle of the sitting monarch when court was open was easy enough, but sticking around... that might be a tall order indeed. Maybe if I could befriend someone on the staff or trick them into thinking I was new, they would help me out.

But luck was against me that day. While the markets were bustling outside the walls, the castle gates were closed.

"Now what?" I asked myself, staring around the plaza.

A rotund woman carrying three children along in her wake shoved past me with a glare and a curse, and I stumbled back toward the outer edges of the square, unprepared for the full-contact sport of medieval markets.

"I've got just the thing for a stunning beauty such as yourself," a sleazy voice proffered.

The market stall I'd fled to safety beside was full of dangerous-looking jewelry, a perfect match for the man now leaning over his stall and holding out a brooch with what looked like stained glass shards stuck into a lead setting. The glass, some of which had sharp edges and potentially blood from customers that should've looked, not touched, shone dully, in need of a polish.

"That's far too beautiful, I couldn't possibly do it justice." I said, turning to find a more secluded spot to plan my next steps.

"Nonsense!" He lowered the brooch and placed it back on the table. "If this doesn't catch your fancy, perhaps some of my other pieces will."

"No, thank you." A break opened in the crowd, and across the plaza was a small alley leading between the castle ramparts and another sectioned-off area. I hurried through, the crowds filling in again in my wake. It was so narrow that the late afternoon sun wasn't doing much to illuminate it, but once my eyes adjusted, I continued forward. I didn't sense anything dangerous this way. On the contrary, I had that familiar tug in the pit of my stomach that always guided me toward the things I was seeking.

Coming out on the other side, I regathered my bearings. It looked like I was inside the castle ramparts now, but why would they have an unprotected alleyway where anybody could waltz in?

Suddenly conscious of getting caught, I turned to conceal myself back in the alley, but it wasn't there. My breathing quickened as I hurried along the wall, feeling exposed and waiting for the castle guard to swoop in. Could I have conjured that alley from another time where it existed? I'd never overlaid a different time period on another, but the other big lesson I'd learned was that when it came to time, nothing was certain, and anything was possible.

Ahead of me was an iron gate partially open to a grassy courtyard with lots of long shadows to hide in if necessary. There was nobody in sight, so I kept moving. Halfway across, I realized this was the courtyard I saw when I first tracked Arthur here. At least I knew I was still in the right place.

Voices up ahead made me pause, and I flattened myself back against the wall, wishing I could do glamour magick or even conjure an invisibility cloak of some kind. I was pretty sure those were real, anyway. I didn't know many magi personally, so they were almost mythical in my mind.

Damn, I was sheltered growing up, even from other Strangers. There were so many things I didn't know about the world I was a part of.

Focus, Meg. Gripe about your past later.

Two men came into view, each carrying a satchel full of tools and covered in dust. I inched farther away from them, but they were too absorbed in their conversation to notice the weirdo hiding in the shadows.

"Do you think they'll make good on their word? We've been busting our asses to get this built on time."

The other man grunted. "I don't know. It always sounds too good to be true when nobles promise extra anything, especially pay." He scratched at his beard. "Arthur did say they were good for it though. I trust him."

The first man nodded his agreement. "Never let us down, yet." He chuckled. "Agnes's birthday is coming up. It'd be nice to get her something of quality for once."

"Of all the things you could spend the extra money on, and you pick a present for your daughter?" He sounded both disgusted and amused. "I don't understand you."

The men continued ribbing each other until they were out of earshot. They sounded sincere when they were talking about Arthur, but what did they really know? It didn't take much to fool people, especially since he could blame it on those holding the purse strings if it didn't work out.

It didn't matter, anyway. I was sending him back to the lodge and the prison waiting for him one way or the other. He could plead his case to Bel. Decent person or no, if he was the Desma I thought he was, his fate was sealed.

I didn't notice the person behind me until there was a tap on my shoulder. I froze, but relaxed somewhat when the voice that spoke wasn't that of an angry guard.

"Miss, are you supposed to be here?"

I turned to find a mousy young woman, in her late teens. She was wearing the plain garb of a servant and had her plain brown hair pulled into a tight bun that added severity to her plain face. But there was a shrewdness in her eyes and a set of her shoulders that spoke of danger hidden in plain sight.

This woman was a Stranger and the face she wore was a disguise. And from the way she was regarding me, she knew she hadn't stumbled across a hapless, lost human.

"Probably not," I smiled. "But maybe you can help me."

Chapter Five

Genevieve was the best possible person that I could've run across. By the time night fell, the fae woman had me set up with the laundresses, bewitching them so they'd believe that I was her cousin and had been hired on.

"I don't want anything from you," she'd said, when I'd asked her price for helping me.

"You don't even know why I'm here," I replied, incredulous.

A hint of her true nature peeked through, and I saw a feral, beautiful spirit unconcerned with the troubles of others. She shrugged with a mischievous smile, gray eyes crinkling in the corners.

"I don't need to. You're interesting." As if that explained everything, she gave me a wink and walked away.

A restless night spent tossing and turning on the straw cot that was many months overdue for a change led into a long morning of mindless dunking and scrubbing a large castle's-worth of laundry. I kept waiting for an opportunity to slip away, but nothing appeared until the matriarch of the group, Helga, sent me off on a delivery.

Basket in my arms, I set off for the banquet hall—wherever that was—to drop off fresh-pressed table linens. The castle was bustling with activity and I enjoyed wandering. As long as I looked like I had a destination to get to, nobody paid me any mind.

I walked through the grand entry hall and glimpsed the throne room, shuttered and dark, but I could see enough of the tapestries and the thrones themselves that I'd have plenty of new things to share with Bel when I returned.

Now, smart money would have had the banquet hall around here somewhere, but I hadn't yet found it. Finally, after realizing I'd been gone for too long already, I caught the eye of a woman that was passing by.

"Pardon, I'm new here. Could you tell me where the banquet hall is?"

The woman smiled brightly. "Of course. I'm headed that way, too."

I sighed with relief. "Perfect."

She eyed my laundry basket. "Helga send you?"

I nodded, and she tutted. "She tricked you."

"What do you mean?"

The woman appraised me from the corner of her eye. "She always sends the new girls to the 'banquet hall.' You had the right idea. The feasting hall is here." The woman pointed at a set of magnificent double doors with gold-inlaid pastoral scenes over the entire surface. "But when she says banquet hall she just means the family's usual dining chamber."

"Oh. Then I don't feel bad about being gone so long," I said.

"Nor should you." She shook her head and grinned. "I don't know why she finds so much joy in her little game."

"It's the only fun she gets," I said solemnly. "The frown lines on her face look older than she is."

The woman laughed, and I joined in.

"What's your name?" she asked.

"Meg."

"Lovely to meet you, Meg. I'm Sasha."

"That's a beautiful name. It's nice to meet you."

We turned the corner into a narrower hallway and some of the hustle and bustle died away. Stern-faced older staff members eyed us contemptuously as we passed. Sasha and I would whisper jokes about them and giggle like schoolgirls. I couldn't remember the last time I'd met such an immediately likable person.

We next crossed through an open-air walkway that overlooked a larger courtyard than the one I'd found myself in the day I arrived. Across the way I could see builders hard at work on a new structure, the stone walls already well on their way to completion with signs that the wooden roof would be underway soon. Already the carpenters had tooled some ornate cornices that were set aside, waiting for their time to shine.

"My husband is leading that project," Sasha said, her cheeks reddening.

Judging by her reaction I took a wild guess. "Newlyweds?"

Her cheeks flushed even deeper, but she shook her head. "We've been married for a couple of years, but he always makes me feel like I'm newly in love with him. And the way that he looks at me—like I'm his whole world."

I smiled. "That's wonderful. You've got your fairy tale."

Sasha giggled. "I guess I do." She gasped and looped her arm through mine. "You should join us for dinner sometime! Arthur would love to meet you."

A bucket of ice water being tossed in my face would have been less shocking. Sasha noticed my tension and looked at me warily. "Is something the matter?"

I stammered before I found my words again. "No." I sought frantically for an excuse. "It's just that you've been so kind. Most people just look at me suspiciously."

Her concern melted away into another bright smile. "I'm sure they'll warm up to you. Except for the elders. They look at all of us like that."

We laughed again and fell back into our easy stroll.

"So what do you say? Will you come by for dinner?"

"I'd love to. I'm not sure when, I'm still being run pretty ragged as the new girl. But maybe in the next week or so?"

"That would be lovely."

It wasn't long before we reached the dining hall, so I wasn't able to extract much more information about Arthur, other than she was truly in love with him. The one thing that was very clear was that this was going to be more difficult than I thought.

The next few days went by in a blur. I became a stalker, watching for Arthur, asking people about him, trying to find something that would mean he was the monster I suspected. Doubt was pulling at me stronger by the day as I second guessed the decision to send a good man to a prison. And what about Sasha?

I needed him to be detestable, someone worthy of the fate I was about to sentence him to. A couple of times I'd hidden around a corner to listen to him talk to someone, but after the head butler demanded, loud enough for the entire hall to turn and stare, "What in God's name do you think you're doing!" I gave that up.

I kept putting Sasha off with excuses. She was so kind, and I hated hurting her feelings, but I couldn't risk it. The biggest shame is that if we'd met in my time, I think we'd have been best friends, something I never had growing up.

Still didn't, really. Bel always had something or other to fill my time with. He was a bit single-minded that way, but it's the reason he's so good at keeping all this going.

What the hell was I supposed to do? None of this made sense. Arthur seemed like a kind and generous person. His wife adored him, people respected him. Not once had I seen him raise his voice or say an unkind word about anyone, even when people were hassling him.

This wasn't how it was supposed to be. Monsters, and the people they took into their ranks, were heartless, evil. You could feel the slime oozing out of them and trying to infect you with its wickedness. At least, that's what I thought.

I still had to drop off a basket of towels in the kitchen before I called it a day. Then I could find a tavern and all the various things to distract me within it. The lower corridors were a maze, and I was keeping careful watch for the details I'd memorized to find the way.

The bent torch bracket. Turn left.

Crack on the bottom corner pane of glass. Another left.

The cobblestone that sticks up enough to—I cursed—trip over. Turn right.

The smell of the abattoir. Go straight.

So focused was I on the guideposts that I collided with a solid object and almost went toppling backward onto my ass, but a hand wrapped around my arm and caught me. The linen basket tumbled out of my grip and I rushed to pick them up before they gathered any of the perpetual grime that no amount of sweeping or mopping would clean off the floors.

"I'm sorry, are you alright?" I mumbled, not looking away from my task. The roadblock didn't answer, but had stooped to help me pick up the mess, and I cast a quick, annoyed glance in their direction. I choked on my own spit and started to cough violently when I saw Arthur looking back at me, concerned.

I hastily turned away, fighting to get the coughing under control. When I turned back around, Arthur had the basket neatly refolded and waiting, a confused smile on his face.

"Thank you." I reached for the basket, but he didn't relinquish it, tucking it under his arm instead.

He blinked and I could tell he was searching for words, still trying to figure something out. "You're a new face. I think I've seen you a couple of times, but we haven't been introduced. I'm Arthur."

I bowed my head. "Nice to meet you, sir." I reached for the laundry again, but he twisted it away.

"And your name is?"

My eyes narrowed, annoyance creeping in again. "Meg. Now I really must be going, I have my chores."

The smile grew on his face. "You're not the same Meg that my wife keeps talking about, are you?"

I played dumb. "Who's your wife?"

"Sasha." The glitter in his eyes said I wasn't fooling him, but he dropped the subject. "Which way are you headed?"

"Kitchens," I sighed, walking away without waiting to see if he was following. I slowed my pace to walk alongside him when his gaze burning into me was too much.

"What brings you here?" he asked.

"I needed employment."

He nodded genially. "And you're a new laundress?"

I gazed balefully at the basket he refused to relinquish. "Clearly." Being this close to him brought a dangerous heat to my belly.

He stopped. "The odd thing is, they don't allow people to work in the castle unless they're sent from reputable families with a record of service. The only thing anyone seems to know is that you're the cousin of one of the girls here. But she has a way of pulling the wool over people's eyes." Arthur still seemed amicable enough, but a hint of suspicion shone in his eyes.

I cocked my head to the side. So he'd been doing his homework the same as I had. He must've sensed me after all. "I assure you, I'm very trustworthy. And Genevieve may be fae"—I looked him right in the eye as I said it—"but she's just trying to help."

"Well, that settles it." Arthur handed me the basket and as I grabbed it, he placed his hand over mine. A sudden fire blazed through me as our magicks flared. Arthur's eyes sharpened to a hard edge before knowing blasted across his face in a sudden epiphany.

Without another word, he turned and walked away. My chest heaved as I fought to catch my breath. Emotions welled up that I had no business feeling toward him. Could that have been a power of his? Manipulation by touch? What else could trigger a reaction that strong?

After the initial shock wore off, the flare of desire took its place, stronger than it had ever been before. But where it had always manifested as an unbridled lust in the past, this was different. A new fire blazed and tore through me, leaving me aching in heart, body, and soul. As I stared at the spot on my hand that Arthur had touched, there was a sense of hunger accompanying the lust. A sense that where I'd been left unsatisfied in the past, that man would be the one to sate me.

It had to be a trick.

I struggled to push the pangs aside as I dropped off the laundry, the heat of the kitchens actually feeling cooler than my skin when I walked through the door. I just needed to finish this up and I could escape, get some fresh air, try to find relief, and figure out what the fuck was going on here.

Chapter Six

The next day, I was much more wary about my attempts. I couldn't get over the intensity of just a brief touch of his skin. The sorcerers and sycophants I'd captured before—granted there weren't that many—had been terrible people. They didn't even attempt to hide it.

A sorcerer, complete with pointed mustache and sharply-shaped eyebrows, second in severity only to his widow's peak, was twisting his hands in glee when I'd found him. He boasted about all the magick he'd worked for the Titans, all the sacrifices he'd offered, how he couldn't wait to meet them and take his place beside them.

I transported him to the lodge with no further inquiry just to shut him up.

How could I get Arthur to show his true colors?

Sasha barreled over to me as I was coming off a back staircase with another delivery. I'd shown no irritation at Helga's little prank, so now she was sending me all over the castle with increasingly vague directions just to see if I would crack. Worked just fine for me, of course. More time to snoop.

"Meg, perfect timing!" She grabbed my basket under her arm and grabbed my hand. "Come with me!"

"Where are we going?" I sputtered, letting her drag me along.

We turned a corner to where Arthur was waiting. He locked eyes with me and stole the breath from my lungs.

"This is the woman I've been telling you about," she said.

Arthur smiled and tipped his head in a small bow. "I've heard so much about you, I feel like I know you already."

"It's nice to meet you." My voice was breathy, but I played along, not knowing where he was going with this. My pulse had already quickened, and I felt a heat coming off him. Or maybe that was me.

"Tell Meg that it's no bother at all to join us for dinner. We'd love her company."

Arthur nodded. "Indeed. We have plenty to go around. Sasha and I love to share our good fortune with others."

Sasha beamed. "Can you believe it? Humble and generous? Have you ever heard of such a thing from an accomplished tradesman?" Sasha wasn't posturing to humble brag. Her admiring gaze at her husband said it all.

Arthur wrapped his arm around Sasha and kissed the top of her head. "She gives me more credit than I deserve." He stared down at her and I could see the love that he had for her. That was when an emotion I didn't expect wriggled to the surface. Jealousy.

This whole situation felt wrong. I envisioned myself taking Sasha's position, no matter that I adored this woman and wouldn't dream of hurting her.

"Meg!"

I turned to the angry voice behind me to find Helga standing there.

"Why haven't you delivered that basket yet, you lazy fool," she snapped, her hand slicing in a cutting motion toward the basket still in Sasha's arm.

Arthur stepped in with the save. "Apologies, Helga, we distracted her. I wanted to meet the woman that's become such fast friends with my wife."

Helga's face softened when she looked at Arthur. "Ah. How is the new hall coming along?"

"Just fine, thank you."

She nodded, all traces of kindness evaporating from her face as her eyes swiveled back around to me. "Get a move on, girl."

I nodded, grateful for the interruption. Sasha handed me my basket with a guilty smile, and I scurried off.

There were a couple more deliveries to run still, and my feet were aching. I'd switched to the soft-soled slippers I'd borrowed from Genevieve and hidden my leather boots away, but I was paying for my stubborn desire for historical anachronism now.

After dropping off my second to last delivery, I spotted a quaint bench being warmed in the sun and gave in to the demands of my feet.

"You can wait, Helga," I grumbled, taking a seat. I inhaled a few deep breaths, thankful that the wind was in the ideal direction to carry the smell of the surrounding city away.

I closed my eyes for a moment, just to organize my thoughts, when a shadow fell over me.

"Who are you? Really?"

I cracked my eyes open and looked at Arthur, looming over me with determination. His arms, corded with muscle from years of heavy labor, crossed tightly over his chest.

"A traveler." Nice. Keep it noncommittal.

"From where?"

"A different time."

He nodded and said the last words I expected to come out of his mouth. "Makes sense, for a child of Kronos."

I stared at him, mouth agape. "How—"

"I spent three-hundred years fighting at the side of the Titans. I know their energy when I feel it. The minute I touched your hand the other day, I knew."

"Why didn't you say anything, then?"

Frustration worked its way into his stance, making him fidget. "I wasn't expecting it. It brought a lot of things back."

"Things like what?" I tried to keep the keen interest out of my voice and failed. I had my fingers crossed that he would say something awful.

A ghost of a smile crossed his face and his eyes shifted to some faraway point. He sat down heavily on the edge of the bench, as far away from me as possible.

"Let's start with why you're here," he insisted, fixing me with a stare that cut through me. I'd never felt so exposed from a glance. Heat pooled in my core, despite my attempts to quash it with thoughts of him in direct contact with the monsters I hated most.

He fought by their side. The gods only knew how much damage he'd done, how many innocent people he'd killed.

But I couldn't make myself believe it. I sighed. "I like to jump around. Something pulled me here, so I thought it'd be a fun place to visit."

His reply was instantaneous and dark with warning. "Don't lie to me."

"That's the only answer you're getting," I said, setting my jaw in determination.

"At least tell me who sent you. Was it them?"

The Titans? Why would they have anything to do with it? But it gave me an idea of how I could get the answers I was seeking.

I answered simply. "Yes."

My hope that it would elicit the response I needed, showing his true colors, fell apart then. Instead, his eyes softened and happiness leached into his gaze. He reached out a hand and brushed his fingers along my jaw. "I'd given up hope. I never thought you'd come."

His thumb brushed my lower lip, and I moaned as the heat at my core flared brightly, consuming every part of me. Arthur slid closer on the bench, his hand resting on my knee.

"How are the others? Have you bonded yet?"

My head swam as I got lost in the joy in his eyes. "I—"

His hand moved to cup my cheek, and he leaned in. He smelled of musk, earth, and oak, and the scent pushed all other thoughts aside. Our mouths brushed together, his tongue running along my bottom lip. I wanted so badly to fall for his lies.

"I—" What had I been trying to say? He'd asked me a question, hadn't he?

Arthur's fingers moved into my hair and he held me there as he kissed me. I could feel him resonating within me, like we'd begun to share a heartbeat. It was consuming and entangling and heady. I'd never experienced anything like it.

He broke away, panting. "Does this mean you're ready?"

The feel of his lips still hypnotized me. Dreamily, I asked, "Ready for what?"

Arthur stilled and pulled away. I tried to follow, but he held me at arm's length.

His suspicion was sharp and the coldness coming off him jerked me out of my euphoria. "You aren't here at their behest, are you?"

"Arthur, I—"

He pushed me away and got to his feet, hurrying down the hall.

"Wait, please!" I called.

Arthur stilled. He was fighting the instinct to turn around, but his shoulders set, and he took a heavy step forward before continuing down the hall and out of sight.

Everything in me wanted to run after him, to try to explain. The hunger that had been ready to feast on gentle caresses, words whispered against bare skin, drops of sweat, gasps and moans turned on me in an instant, leaving me empty with a gnawing loneliness. It didn't linger or leave me aching. It left me utterly alone.

Chapter Seven

I needed to think things over, mainly what my connection was with Arthur. There was no doubt in my mind that he was one of the elite Desma. So was his effect on me part of his power? Was it because I was a construct and it was preprogrammed that I would be drawn to the elite to accomplish the Titans' plans? There weren't many better ways to manipulate someone than going straight for the heart.

Even Bel didn't elicit these kinds of feelings in me, and he was the man I loved.

I clutched my stomach and grimaced, the sensation a telltale sign that I was lying to myself. The sensation redoubled as I spiraled into denial, but I wouldn't give in. It had to be a trick. It had to be.

For the rest of the day, I laid low. I couldn't go back to my quarters because that's the first place Helga or Sasha would think to look for me. So I explored while I pulled my thoughts together.

Eventually my feet led me to the worksite that Arthur was managing. Everyone had gone home for the day and darkness was starting to creep in, leaving long shadows over the interior as I picked my way carefully through the trip hazards around the building before stealing through an open doorway, the frame fitted and waiting to be completed.

It was nice and quiet, and the thick stone walls trapped in the cool air. Crickets started to chirp from the corners, and I took a seat in an open window frame on the back of the building, facing the castle wall so chances were slim I'd be seen.

The breeze whispering through the uncovered wooden beams of the roof and the chirps of birds settling in for the evening joined with the crickets to make a soothing background. I leaned my head against the smooth stone wall and closed my eyes.

When I opened them again, Arthur was standing a few feet away.

I started and pitched backward, rolling out of the window and popping back to my feet. Arthur followed, taking cautious steps as he climbed over the ledge, hands out to calm my fears. My back bumped into the wall and he stopped.

His words were kind and somewhat sad. "It's clear you have no idea who you are."

That grated on me. "Excuse me?"

"Who sent you here? Did someone get to you?"

"Nobody got to me—"

Arthur took a step forward, his patience giving way to a hint of mania. "I need you to tell me the truth." He reached for me but let his hand drop. "Please. Tell me the truth."

"I am telling the truth. Nobody sent me here. It was my choice. I found you because of your link to the Titans—"

"You found me because of your link to me." He was becoming desperate, running his hands through his hair and pacing back and forth. "At least tell me what your intentions are."

I never should have investigated this far into it. "I was only trying to determine the kind of person you were. I don't know what your abilities are but you're clearly adept at some kind of manipulation."

Arthur turned on me, offended. "I've done no such thing. That's our connection, which you'd know if someone else hadn't interfered in your destiny."

"What destiny? Jail breaking the Titans from Tartarus? Letting them destroy the world or bring it under their thumb? I never should have doubted myself. You're all the same, Bel was right."

Arthur crossed the space between us and got right in my face, his breath boiling on my skin. "Belsioch?"

Chills ran down my spine. Had I said too much? But not answering was all the answer he needed.

Arthur cursed and picked up a chunk of wood, throwing it so hard against the stone it exploded into splinters. "Belsioch is the enemy! How long has he been brainwashing you!"

I stared at him in his rage. This was the proof I'd been waiting for. "The only enemy here is you." I strode forward, calling the currents of time to me. He could feel it roiling in the air and he looked around wildly as I put my hand firmly on his chest.

Arthur put his hand over mine, eyes pleading. "Don't do this. Whatever he told you, it's lies."

An icy glare is all I replied with.

As the currents rose, Arthur squeezed my hand tenderly, a look of longing on his face. "Please."

I closed the currents around him and sent him through time, to the lodge and the holding cell. He disappeared, and I followed, taking a path far different from his.

Arthur's eyes still haunted me as I trudged up the driveway. I'd needed to decompress before I spoke to Bel, so I traveled back into my current time in the woods outside our home. My head was all kinds of twisted up. Bel would probably be angry that I'd put myself through the ringer just to prove him right in the end.

The door opened and a rectangle of light spilled out onto the walkway.

"You did it."

I looked up at Bel, his face lit with a smile, which I tentatively returned.

"You caught a big fish," he continued, meeting me halfway and scooping me into his arms. I tried to relax into him like I always did, but I wasn't able to work the tension out of my shoulders.

Bel's hands worked up and down my back as he held me, trying to ease worries I couldn't let him know I had. Not all of them, anyway.

He tilted my face up to his and placed a light kiss on my lips, quickly deepening it and wrapping his hands in my hair. My fingers curled into his shirt but I just didn't have the energy. Then my stomach dropped as I realized it wasn't just energy, but desire that wasn't there.

Bel pulled away and searched my face. "What happened out there?"

I shook my head. "I'm still trying to figure it out."

After a long, hot bath, I felt a little more like myself again. We settled on the couch with dinner and a strong pot of coffee before I launched into my story. I told him about Arthur's ability to manipulate and fool people into thinking he was such a great guy. About the lust that he stirred up inside me.

"It's not a surprise," said Bel, stroking my face. "Risha confirmed he's an elite. You should be proud of yourself. You discovered new challenges that we weren't aware of, and you won." His eyebrows creased in concern. "I just hope it didn't cause you too much pain."

"It was a mindfuck, but I'll be alright. I'm not even that horny, believe it or not."

"So you had direct contact with him, but you're not worked up?"

"No. Maybe I was just too angry with his bullshit?"

Bel considered it. "Possibly. What was he telling you?"

"Oh, what you'd expect. The Titans are the good guys, there are so many things I don't know about them, etc."

There was no way I was mentioning anything he'd said about bonding and mates. Or how he almost had me convinced.

I called it an early night after that and went up to bed, but sleep was impossible. Every time I tried to close my eyes, Arthur was looking back at me. Only this time I felt fear, pain, and sorrow. I must've dozed off at one point because he even appeared to me in a dream, saying it wasn't my fault, I didn't know the truth. He forgave me and would miss getting the chance to know me. And he pleaded with me not to hand the others over to Bel. He said they would protect me.

And then he was gone, and I was lying in a heap of rumpled sheets and a pool of sweat.

I gave up on sleep and took a cold shower, my skin feeling feverish after that nightmare. Bel must've been at the lodge, so I went for a run to try to clear my head.

The morning air was crisp, and sunrise was still over an hour away when I set out. Our tiny town was a picturesque masterpiece, every cozy house and garden a pristine example of country living. Even in the dark, the wrought-iron lampposts cast enough of a glow on the streets to make it magickal. Now that summer was on its way, the village would plant more flowering vines along the lights' bases to add to the curb appeal.

I set a comfortable pace, planning at the outset to take a nice slow tour of the entire village. A couple hours of exercise would have me right back to normal. With music blaring in my ears, it made it even easier to block out the intrusive thoughts.

Several blocks had idled by, and I was approaching the side of the village closest to the trails heading up into the mountains. I glanced over and saw a shape moving through the trees. It wasn't unusual. One of my more annoying "gifts" was the ability to see ghosts, something that was strengthened by all my time in the underworld.

I kept running and ignored it. Most of the time the wanderers out here were just echoes, not sentient beings, stuck in a loop of their last days or hours. In the mountains, people experienced all sorts of horrible deaths, so I didn't even take the time to chat with the sentient ones.

As I passed over the curve of the road that ran alongside that sections of trees, a snapping sound made me look up. My toe caught the curb, and I pitched forward, tumbling through the dewy grass. I sat there, watching open-mouthed as Arthur stepped out of the trees.

"How did you escape?" I asked.

Arthur didn't answer, just looked at me with a grieved stare. Then I realized he was transparent.

"What happened?"

He still didn't answer. Arthur raised his hand in a farewell wave, smiling sadly as he dissolved into the shadows.

Had I sent him to his death?

When Bel returned home, he found me sitting at the kitchen table, clutching a mug of tea and deep in thought. I started when he leaned in to kiss the top of my head.

"What's wrong?" he asked.

My eyes never left my tea. "Something keeps nagging at me, and I can't get my mind off it."

"How can I help?" asked Bel.

I hesitated, trying to think of how to phrase it so I wouldn't sound accusatory. "The people that I send through..."

When I didn't continue, Bel prompted, "What about them?"

"Where are they kept?"

Bel's eyes narrowed. "You know where." His head tilted up and to the side, a predatory pose that made me shiver with an inkling of fear. "What are you really asking?"

"I'd like to speak to Arthur. I think that would help me focus on the task."

"He's a threat. He's been imprisoned where he can't do any harm. I'm not letting you near him so he can continue to mess with your head. Just talk to me, let me help you."

"I'm not sure this is something you'll understand." The words were harsher than I intended, and I blanched. "Not in the same way, anyway."

Bel's body was rigid, and his hands were shaking. "Well, then I guess you'll have to figure it out on your own. You're not seeing him." He turned away and stalked off down the hall.

I followed after him. "Because you won't let me, or because I can't?"

Bel whirled on me in a flash. "What are you implying?"

My body tried to betray me and flinch away, but I held my ground. "Did you really go to all the trouble of creating a special prison?" Now that I'd said the words out loud, it sounded childish. I'd let him sell me a fairy tale. "Or did you neutralize the problem in another way?"

Bel drew himself up to his full height, but he didn't stop there. He shed his human form and morphed into the Ætherim he was as I watched, my body quaking.

A huge pair of wings punched holes into the plaster as they demanded more space than the hallway would allow, his clothing shredded away around his thickly muscled body and his hands clenched in front of me, each of them the size of a hub cap. He was doubled over at the waist, hovering over me with his back crushed against the ceiling.

The walls shook when he spoke, his voice a dangerous, low rumble. "Are you accusing me of being a murderer?"

"I'm accusing you of not telling me the truth." I clamped my legs together to stop my knees from shaking.

"I have never lied to you, Meg. Even your brief interaction with that Desma has you so twisted around you don't even trust me. This is the damage he's already done. Why would I let you see him!" he roared. Plaster dust fell from the ceiling, and I heard items falling and shattering in the surrounding rooms.

I flinched as his hands opened and closed into tight fists and he paused. Slowly, he shrunk back down to his human size.

"I'm sorry. I didn't want to scare you, I just—" He ran a hand through his hair. "Hearing you say things like that makes me realize how dangerous these next steps will be. I can't bear the thought of you turning against me."

My knees were still shaking, but I took a tentative step forward and placed my palm on his cheek. "I'm not turning against you. But I think we need to both acknowledge that there are things you aren't telling me. Whether it's because you think you're protecting me or because you think I don't need to know... that doesn't matter. What does matter is that we don't hide things from each other."

A cruel glint edged into Bel's eyes. "Fine. If you tell me with all honesty why you want to speak to Arthur and what has you so worried, we can talk about a visit."

My jaw set so hard, my teeth squeaked. "That seems like an ultimatum, not a sharing of truths."

"I'm starting to doubt your dedication to this mission. If you can't put that pissant out of mind and find the next target, you need to take a long look at yourself before you come to me with accusations."

"My dedication?" I asked, livid now. "I'm asking a few questions, and you're refusing to answer! I thought we were a team?"

"I thought so too." Bel's lip curled. "But I think you've got a stronger Titan's temperament than you want to admit."

"What did you say?" My blood was already rushing in my ears so maybe I hadn't heard him right. "Because surely you aren't implying what I think you are."

"Their blood runs in your veins. I don't think it's too much of a stretch of the imagination that their grip on you would tighten eventually. You were a ticking time bomb. It just took a little longer than they'd imagined for their control on you to set in."

Rage boiled over. "I'm nothing like them! I will never be like them! They don't control me!"

"Prove it!" he raged back. "Carry on with your work, and I'll carry on with mine."

"Oh, I'll carry on. I'll do you one better than that. How about I find them all? Huh? All at once?"

A look akin to panic crossed his face then. "Now, hold on. If you overextend yourself you're no good to anyone either. And you'll light up like a damn beacon and lead the Titans right to you. Are you trying to make it easy for them?"

"What does it matter if I'm already under their control?" I snapped.

He grimaced. "I'm sorry. That was a low blow. But what you're thinking of doing is dangerous. Why risk it?"

"To put to rest any doubt in your mind. I've been playing around with different methods of trance. If I can go deep enough, then—"

"No!"

My mouth snapped shut involuntarily.

"Please," he tried again, breathing hard. "No." He chewed his lower lip, a new behavior for him.

"I didn't want to tell you—" He gave me an apologetic smile and waved his hands to ward off the argument that could easily be made to my point. "—but Risha noticed a serious uptick in energies surrounding you when you located Arthur in your trance at the lodge. You caught someone's attention.

"For the safety of all of us and this mission, we need to keep it as simple as possible, and as quick as possible. From now on, trust your gut. If you find a Desma, send them back. Don't bother with the due diligence. Risha and Ursal can handle it. If it was a mistake, we can rectify it later. No harm, no foul."

"But if I—"

"Meg, please," he said, through clenched teeth. "Trust me." Bel put his hands on my shoulders, pleading. "Do you trust me?"

I stared at him. "Just because I have doubts about some things, doesn't mean I don't trust you."

He smiled and drew me in for an embrace. "I'm glad to hear that." His palm slid to the back of my neck and my skin grew warm, then hot.

I yelped and tried to pull away, but his grip was solid. My head felt fuzzy and my whole body, weightless. "What are you—what are you doing?" My words were slurred.

As my vision narrowed to pinpricks, I heard Bel say, "You'll thank me for this someday."

Chapter Eight

I stretched, luxuriating in the soft bedding that wrapped me up like a cocoon. The birds were singing, a light breeze was blowing through the open window and it was the perfect temperature. On top of all that, I'd had my most restful night's sleep in a long time.

My feet slapped across the cold tile as I entered the kitchen where Bel had breakfast going. He handed me a steaming mug of coffee and sat me down before setting a full plate in front of me.

"Have fun last night?" he asked. "I know I did."

My body flushed at the memory of our long session of lovemaking.

"I did. I should get beat up by minotaurs more often." I leaned over and kissed him, tasting the remnants of strawberry jam on his lips. "Does Risha have any more information on that chalice I brought back?"

I picked up the newspaper and scanned the headlines. Bel was old-fashioned. He even paid extra for it to be delivered since we were the only ones around here who still got the physical paper.

"Nothing yet, but it looks like it might've been a dud. Possibly just used in some kind of ritual to the Titans, but not by them personally."

"Damn," I hissed, angry at myself for another failure. "Next time. I'll get something good, I promise."

Bel smiled at me over his mug. "I have no doubt."

The date on the paper caught my eye. "Wait, is that right? It's Friday?"

For a brief second, Bel's shoulders stiffened. "Yes, that's right. Why?"

"When did I come back? Did I overshoot it?"

"You might've been a bit off the mark, but you were back the same day you left."

"I'm never that far off. I traveled to Crete on Monday."

Bel shook his head. "I don't think it was Monday." He gently slid the newspaper from my hands. "You're still a little tired, how about we have a relaxing day today? We can do whatever you want."

"No," I said, slowly, shaking my head as I thought. "I know it was, because Yvonne brought the meat pies the previous day, on her way home from Sunday services."

"What does it matter?" asked Bel, lightly. "You've been working hard, you're allowed to get time a little jumbled."

"My time doesn't get jumbled," I said. That much I was very confident in. "Did something happen?"

Bel made a noncommittal noise in the back of his throat.

"Bel, did something happen?"

He sighed. "You slept for three days."

"What?" It wasn't a question of alarm. I could tell he was lying to me.

"I'm sure it's nothing to worry about."

"Then why did you ask if I had fun last night?"

Bel faltered and leaned forward. "I didn't want to scare you. Your body just needed to recover." He placed his hand on the back of my neck and leaned in for a kiss. "We're getting close to ending this. It'll become more taxing the closer we get, but we'll lock them away forever." His lips crashed with mine and the skin on my neck got hot under his touch. My whole body eased and all the tension melted away. Why did I always have to worry about everything?

He removed his hand and stood. "Now, what would you like to do today, m'lady?"

The day was a blur. I'd suggested sitting on the couch and binging a show, but Bel suggested all these things we'd talked about doing before, but never got around to. He remembered the weirdest things and our day ended up with a full itinerary. It was fun and exhausting and much needed stress relief.

But a thought kept nagging at me; I couldn't shake it. Like there was a little blip in my memory, something I was forgetting that was really important. I even checked my calendar, but I didn't have any appointments or anything like that.

When we were in the car and the conversation had died down, giving me time to watch out the window and daydream a bit, it would feel like I was on the verge of remembering. Then it would slip away again.

"Want to make a pit stop at the pub on the way home?" Bel offered.

"No." I smiled tiredly. "I'm fine."

All I wanted to do was crawl into bed. Maybe I'd dream about whatever was bothering me so much.

"I tired you out, huh?" he asked with a chuckle.

"Today was great. I can't remember the last time we did something fun together."

Bel took my hand and pressed it to his lips. "Pretty soon, we'll have all the time in the world for each other."

I rolled my eyes. "No pun intended?"

He snorted, proud of himself. "I didn't even mean to make a joke! Damn, I'm good."

"You sure are, babe." I patted his shoulder supportively with a derisive shake of my head as we pulled into the driveway.

I tried to watch at least an episode of our current favorite, but my eyes wouldn't stay open. I woke in Bel's arms as he carried me upstairs and set me into bed.

He caressed my cheek. "I'm going to run up to the lodge, but I'll be back by morning."

"Okay. Be careful."

Bel nodded, and I was already asleep by the time the door closed behind him.

My dreams were a swirling mass of confused thoughts and images that felt like real memories. And there was a man whose face continued to appear. My heart twisted when I saw him, and I'd wake up briefly from the shock of sadness before floating back down into dreams and repeating the process all over again.

After another round of this, my eyes snapped open. "Arthur," I breathed. His name was Arthur. I'd tracked him down in medieval Germany and stalked him to learn the truth. A truth I still wasn't sure about. And then sent him to the lodge, after which I was pretty sure I saw his ghost.

And when I'd confronted Bel about it, we'd had a fight and then—

I growled. That son of a bitch had done something to me to make me forget. Why would he do that? It certainly didn't win him any points if he'd been trying to convince me I could trust him.

I threw the covers back and stalked to the middle of the room, pulling the duvet and pillows off the bed and building a nest on the floor. Bel may think my plan is a bad idea, but to hell with him.

Trying to find my way into a trance when I was fueled by anger wasn't easy, but I managed. Once I was in the void, it was easier to let go and concentrate on the work at hand. I slipped farther down into the current of time, letting it surround me, feeling it ebb and flow as I floated in the tides.

I sank deep within the currents as I pulled my power around me, setting my targets.

Now.

As before, I tuned into my own signature and cast it out. Instead of manifesting as wispy trails, this time the connections were substantial, glowing gold and pulsing with energy. Within a matter of minutes, I'd latched onto one, a signature just like Arthur's. And then another. And another.

Five glowing spheres throughout time, the elites. I'd found them all.

A slamming car door ripped me out of my trance. The lines unraveled, fraying and dissolving. They rebounded and came at me, wrapping me tightly in a swirling mass of emotions and memories which weren't my own. I struggled to break free.

From far away I could hear the front door open and close and unhurried steps walking through the hall. The sudden lurch of panic broke me loose, and I slammed back into my body.

No matter how angry I was with him, I had no desire to show my hand just yet. I forced myself to my feet and threw the pillows on the bed. Steps began to move up the stairs, still not rushed, but not slow enough to get the covers back on.

The steps were on the landing now. I jumped in bed and arranged the covers over me, and just as the doorknob was turning, I tipped over the side of the mattress onto the floor with a thud.

Bel gasped and hurried over as I popped out of the covers like a prairie dog, looking around me confusedly.

"Did I fall out of bed?"

He crouched down in front of me and I got a whiff of something underneath his aftershave and natural musk that took me a minute to pinpoint. Blood.

"Are you alright?" he said, a light laugh bubbling out of him. He helped untangle me from the sheets before holding out his hand to drag me to my feet.

I fought to swipe my hair out of my face. "Yeah. I didn't realize that was an actual thing that can happen." I forced a laugh. "Maybe that minotaur was chasing me in my sleep."

"I hope not," he said, still in a joking mood. "That sounds horrible."

Bel and I remade the bed and soon after I got comfortable, he joined me, wrapping me tightly in his arms. I tried not to stiffen up, his breath warm on the back of my neck.

His soft snoring filled the room, but I doubted I'd be able to sleep. My mind was still full of everything I'd felt and seen and experienced as I connected to the other Desma.

Maybe some of what Arthur said had been true. His spiel about connections... and he'd mentioned bonding. I'd never heard that spoken of in any context other than mates among shifters. There was something undeniable binding me and the Six. We shared a similar essence, that was clear.

As I sifted through the information that bombarded me, I couldn't help but feel what Arthur was saying made sense. These souls weren't slimy and narcissistic. They were bright and deeply concerned with the worlds they were living in.

They weren't hiding in the shadows, waiting for their moment to seize power again, they were living their lives. My gut clenched. Had I made a terrible mistake?

Just then I felt a tug at the edge of my mind. I reached out to it, tuning in. My body flooded with warmth as I made contact, and I gasped. In my mind's eye a picture started to take shape, a man in a tartan, scars crisscrossing his body, his hair at a tight knot at his nape. His eyes bored into me like he was looking right back at me across time and knew me immediately. One of the Desma had traced me.

His face was so serious, I squirmed under the glare. Bel's arms tightened around me in his sleep and the man in my mind frowned, a subtle curl to his lip. I felt without hearing a low growl emanate from him. The connection broke and I relaxed again in Bel's grip, feeling... guilty.

I extricated myself from Bel's arms and sat at the edge of the bed, staring at the clock. What am I supposed to do, here?

I couldn't go back to sleep, so I decided to go for a run. Luckily, there were no ghosts out to haunt me this time.

"How was your jog?" Bel asked as I came into the kitchen, toweling my hair. "You were gone for a while."

"Couldn't sleep. Probably afraid I'd fall out of bed again." I smiled and grabbed some coffee. "I should just start training for a marathon. Long runs seem to be a habit this week."

"When else did you go for a run?"

Dammit. I forgot he still believed his mind-erase bullshit worked. I turned to the fridge to find something to eat and keep him from seeing the look on my face as I came up with a story.

"Oh, I guess you're right. I couldn't have." I spied a yogurt all the way in the back and reached for it, standing on my tiptoes. "Maybe I dreamed it when I was out for so long."

My fingers grazed the yogurt cup, and I finally snagged it. Curse this short frame.

"Do dream runs count as cardio?" Bel joked. "I'd probably start exercising if it did."

My, wasn't he the comedian? I didn't think I'd ever seen him in this good of a mood first thing in the morning, ever.

"Like you need cardio. You literally have the body of a god."

Bel crossed to the sink to put his cup away in the dishwasher before grabbing me around the waist from behind and pulling me to him. "Flattery will get you everywhere. Keep it coming." He nipped at my earlobe, but instead of inspiring a delicious heat, it only landed sourly. And I could still smell the underlying note of coppery rust.

"Your head doesn't need to get any bigger," I said, patting his cheek a little sharply.

"Maybe not," Bel conceded. He spun me around and pressed his lips to mine, grabbing my hips and pulling me close. "Why don't we go to the club tonight?"

I pulled away and his face pinched with anger before smoothing into a mask of amicability.

"I don't know. I'm not really feeling... dance-y."

"Meg."

My name was spoken in a hushed, dead tone. I turned.

Bel was staring at me with black eyes full of menace. Normally, that would've had me quaking and scrambling to make amends, but not today.

His voice was bitter. "You remember, don't you?"

I planted my feet. "Yes. Your little mind-erase trick didn't work."

"It wasn't a trick."

I crossed my arms and decided better of it. If he came after me again, I was prepared to throw down. "Like hell it wasn't. You tried to erase my fucking memories! After telling me I was just as awful as the Titans? You gaslighting son of a bitch."

My heel squeaked against the marble as I turned and marched for the stairs. Bel's hand circled around my arm with a tight grip and in a move I didn't even think I was capable of, I kicked him in the side of the ribs and, when he released me in surprise, drove my fist into his nose.

"Don't you ever touch me again!" I screamed at his bent form. He looked at me with such anger over the hand clasping his nose that I backed up a step but didn't run. No sense in instigating a predator's instincts.

Bel squared his shoulders and dropped his hand, only a small trickle of blood in one nostril. His long fingers gripped his nose and straightened the cartilage with a crunch. "At least let me explain."

Chapter Nine

"There's nothing more for you to say. Your actions did that for you."

"Meg—"

I clapped my hands together to cut him off. "If you start talking down to me like I'm a goddamn child, I'll rip your dick off."

Bel's head turned on an angle and—he smiled? A grin spread across his thin lips and a rumble in his chest broke into a laugh. I could only stare dumbly at the sight.

Still laughing, he asked, "When did you get so vicious?"

"When my partner, who I thought I could trust, betrayed me in a big way." I'm glad one of us could find the humor in this situation. Not.

The laughter faded, and he became serious. "You have every right to be angry."

"I already know that, but I'm glad you're catching on."

Bel moved to take a seat at the table but thought better of it and headed to the living room. "Please, Meg. Will you let me try to explain?"

Eyes narrowed and not in the slightest convinced that he'd have anything to say that would change my mind, I sat down across from him.

"I'm sorry. I should have told you all of this sooner, but I panicked."

"You panicked?" I asked, deadpan, eyebrows in my hairline.

"There's something you don't know. About why this is affecting you like it is." There was one overarching emotion in his voice and stance—regret.

My resolve softened, just a little, and I eased back in my seat.

"There are so many other ways I tried to come up with that wouldn't put you in direct contact with the Desma. Besides the fact that it's dangerous anyway as your brand of magick doesn't typically aid in battle."

"Don't remind me," I lamented.

He gave a tiny smile and continued. "The closer you get to them—the Titans and the Desma—you become more weaponized."

He let that hang in the air between us, but I only stared.

"You've set off a ticking clock. It's like they just activated their Jason Bourne. Only in your case, there's a strong likelihood that you would be a mindless machine that can also free the Titans." He was so earnest. "I don't want to see you disappear and become the tool you always feared you would be."

Silence settled, thick, in the room.

"Why didn't you tell me this sooner? And why would it be a problem now, and not before? I've had years of contact hunting for the links."

"But they've never been this strong. Arthur said it himself. He worked directly with the Titans, one of their right-hand men. And I'm guessing you found them by tuning in to your own signature?" He crossed his legs and sat back, hands clasped around his knee. Checkmate.

I stared at him coldly. "If you knew all this, we might've devised a way around it. We could've worked out a plan together. If I'd found a different way to track them down—"

"I know. You're right. But I was hoping it wouldn't come to that."

I opened my mouth to call him any number of names, but they died on my tongue as helplessness settled in.

Bel leaned toward me. "It's too little, too late. And again, I am sorry. I thought if I could make you forget Arthur, it would buy me some time to put together a plan. To make it safer to go after the others."

My neck cracked as I whipped my head toward him, incredulous.

He frowned. "We still need to finish this. I know I'm asking a lot of you, and I probably have no right to do so after everything I've put you through already, but we don't have a choice. This must end, with the threat they pose eliminated forever."

That dark pit that I kept locked up tight behind barbed wire and guard dragons started to yawn open beneath me, ready to swallow me up the minute I gave in to the traumas of the past. "And what if they take me over completely? What if I lose myself to their power and become their weapon, and I turn on you? Or the Desma win me over with that connection they have to me? In the moment, their powers of persuasion are... considerable."

My thighs pressed together automatically in the memory of Arthur running his tongue along my bottom lip.

"I'm working on that." Bel reached over and grabbed my hands. "I will find a way to keep you safe. Will you give me another chance?"

His thumbs caressed the backs of my hands, and he seemed for all the world like he was telling me the truth. But I'd believed him before, and look where that got me. If he was telling the truth this time, then it might be too much of a risk to ignore. My instinct was shouting at me, but was it just influenced by my anger at him?

"I need to think about this."

Bel's grip tightened for a moment before he dropped my hands and nodded. "Very well." He stood and grabbed his car keys and jacket from the front hall. "I'll head to the lodge and see what kind of headway I can make with a solution."

He hesitated before walking out the door. "If you have any more questions, please don't hesitate to ask. I'm done trying to hide things from you. I hate seeing you hurt like this, and I hate myself for causing it."

The door clicked shut behind him and a few moments later, I watched the sun glint off the hood of his car as he drove away.

I was stuck between two truths, and had no way of knowing which one was the right one. Just the way Arthur made me feel was enough to make me lean in that direction, but when my libido is going wild, I'm not in the most discerning head space. Sex, or the promise of it, is a great way to control people. It doesn't take an evil genius to know that.

But Bel's truth was much more terrifying. My entire life growing up I'd been told that I was nothing but a vessel, a channel for the power that would free my "family" and let them take control of the world like they always wanted. They'd locked me away, a prisoner in the underworld. The family of Ætherim that were raising me—if you consider doing the bare minimum to keep me alive, "raising"—were using me to gain power when it came time to set the Titans free.

I hadn't been able to make friends because I was isolated. I was educated by the standards of any ancient Strangefells family, which was to say that I'd been taught how to function in high society and the bare minimum of everything else so that I could hold an interesting conversation when they dressed me up and dragged me to dinner parties and galas.

But when I attempted to form my own opinion or try to adopt my own style, I would be punished severely. As I got older, the punishments went from punching and slapping to more extreme methods. The last time I ever crossed them, they threw me into a dark room and starved me for weeks until I was screaming for forgiveness.

I stayed well away from the line and didn't even think about crossing it again. At least not in their presence. I would sneak to the library whenever I could and learn from old spell books and grimoires. I even studied up on the almanacs and the accounting books for the house's expenses. Anything to try to keep my own mind to myself.

The first time they told me what I was, they acted like it was a blessing. My father was one of the most powerful beings in the universe. He could crush entire planets under his will. If he hadn't been betrayed, they never would have captured him and the others, and the world would be a far better place.

He was great and terrible, as were his kin. Someday I would travel to the lower realms of hell and break them free.

I'd asked them what would happen to me, and they'd laughed. You would've thought I'd been doing a great stand-up bit.

You'll be lauded for your sacrifice. Your name will never be forgotten. A high honor.

The very first beating I got was after I said I had no interest in dying for people I didn't even know.

Bel was the one that had saved me from all that. He'd found me and secreted me away. Gave me a home that was safe and loving, introduced me to the twins and helped me build a life, and a mind of my own.

It was my idea to find a way to shut the Titans in Tartarus forever. Let their weapon turn against them. Let their carefully laid plans fall to shit. Let this last betrayal hurt the worst.

Part Two

Chapter Ten

Bel

"**I**'ll do it."

Music to my ears. When Meg walked into the lodge with her confidence returned, I knew this would work. I knew she was on our side.

I drew her into my arms and held her tightly.

"Thank you, love." I pulled away enough to meet her gaze. "I am truly sorry."

She gave me a begrudging smile. "You should be. But I knew it was a bad idea, and we both paid for it. So I'm sorry, too."

I drew her toward the stairs, eager to show her the progress we'd already made. "You have perfect timing. Risha and I might have figured out a work-around."

"I think what he means is, Risha found a work-around while he watched and added commentary." Risha grinned up at us from behind a pile of books, bottles, jars, and sketchy-looking instruments that might've been used in the early days of human medicine.

"Now *that* I believe," said Meg, nudging me playfully in the ribs.

"Okay, enough of that." I motioned for Risha to carry on.

She held up a simple amulet on a silver chain and handed it to Meg, who wrapped her delicate fingers around it and kept it at arm's length as she appraised it.

"It won't bite," said Risha. "Put it on."

"Here, allow me." I held my hand out and Meg passed me the amulet before turning her back to me and lifting her hair. I grazed her neck with my fingers and smiled as she shuddered. The clasp stuck a bit, but I finally got it secured. "There."

Meg fingered the chain thoughtfully. "Is it supposed to be doing something?"

"Not unless you activate it," said Risha. She got to her feet and thumbed a few pages back in a heavy tome before sliding it around for Meg to see. "This is like the force field to end all force fields. Trigger it with a word and press it firmly between two fingers. I've already programmed it for 'Nope', but we can change it if you'd like. It will cut you off from any influence around you."

Risha held up her finger. "But—"

Meg snorted. "Dammit, I hate when there's a but."

"But—" she said again, winking, "—it will also cut off your own energy, which could leave you vulnerable, like if you had to escape quickly."

"The whole idea is to shut off any influence the other Desma might try to exact over you, completely. Part of you is connected to them no matter what we do, but at least this should allow you to separate yourself enough that you can keep a clear head in any situation. And if the Titans try to control you, this should lessen the impact if not block it out entirely."

"So this essentially makes me an autonomous person?" Meg said dryly. She tried to hide her sadness, but not well enough.

"Pretty soon, you will be completely sovereign, in every way."

Meg plucked at the amulet, worrying her lip between her teeth.

"What's on your mind?" I asked, staring at her intently, studying her reactions. She was hiding from me.

"Nothing." She shrugged. "Not much anyway." The question in her eyes told me what was coming before she said it.

"Shouldn't we try this out before I take the risk in the field?"

My hands clenched at my sides, before I took a breath and forced them to loosen. "And how would you propose to do that?"

She turned her head toward the back hallway where the door to the subbasement stood. "It would be the easiest—"

"We've already talked about this. There's no way." My blood boiled at her insolence. How could she continue to question this? Question me?

"Why?" Her hip jutted out to the side as she crossed her arms, ever defiant. "It should just be a quick visit. Try out the amulet, done."

She looked to Risha for support but the nephilim stayed silent, returning to her work. Meg's face fell as she took in Risha's avoidance of the subject.

"Meg, for the last time." I spoke carefully, trying to keep my anger at bay. "Arthur is alive. But you seem to think that it's just a matter of popping into the pocket dimension and back again. It takes far more than that to get in and out, otherwise it wouldn't be a prison."

She winced, and I regretted how condescending it sounded. In my defense, Meg hadn't reached her hundredth year yet. I'd had many millennia on this earth before the Titan wars and many more since. I wasn't used to having to explain things like this.

"But it's still possible," she countered.

I threw my hands in the air with a disgusted grunt. "Enough! It's not happening!" I leaned in toward her, pulse racing. "Here's another truth, since I said I wouldn't lie to you anymore. That prison world isn't for the faint of heart. That place is a vast open plain, much like the underworld, but people tend to forget things much quicker. By now he probably has only a slight idea of who he is, if at all. There are creatures to contend with, as well as the other souls we've locked away, most of whom have probably gone quite mad by now."

She was staring at me with horror etched all over her face, tears in her eyes. I smirked. "You wanted answers. There they are."

"That's terrible," she whispered.

"Your tender heart didn't want us to kill anyone. But if you honestly believed that I would keep them in lives of luxury, you're more gullible than I thought. These people are monstrous. They're lucky they're not in Tartarus where they belong."

"Bel," Risha said quietly, placing her hand on my arm. I yanked it away with a snarl and Meg startled like a scared rabbit, bolting up the stairs.

Risha stood and followed her. "I'll go talk to her." She scowled at me before she disappeared upstairs.

I sat heavily in a chair and massaged my forehead. That hadn't gone how I'd planned.

Chapter Eleven

Meg

I pushed past Ursal as he was coming into the lodge and he grunted with surprise. "What happened?" he called after me as I hurried for the trees.

I didn't answer, just kept heading for my not-so-secret, favorite hideaway and soon disappeared into my sanctuary.

"Meg!" Risha called. "Wait up!"

Slowing my pace only slightly, my muscles soon complained as I climbed a steep tread leading to a cliff overlooking the gully. The swift-moving water had cut between the rocks, the sound bouncing up and surrounding me in the constant rumble. Some birds nesting nearby added to the sweet comfort of the noise and I tucked into a corner, hidden from view.

When Risha's shadow fell over me, she just wordlessly sat and joined me in watching the water, our shoulders touching.

After the silence had stretched on too long even for me, I said ruefully, "Guess I win the award for dumbest idiot."

I heard Risha's light huff of breath before the rumble of the river swallowed it up. "You're not dumb. You're an idealist."

"Code for naïve dummy," I restated.

"Perhaps naïve," she admitted. "But there's nothing wrong with wanting to believe it. You're a good person, who's doing difficult things to save the world from monsters. Bel wanted to spare you the guilt of knowing where people ended up." I felt her shrug. "Apparently he just felt like being an asshole today."

"That's a common occurrence with him, lately."

"Pretty sure it's because he's jealous of Arthur, and the fact that you want to see him so badly."

My eyes almost popped out of my head as I looked at her. Risha continued to stare forward, no sign that she was joking.

"I have a hard time believing that. He's not the jealous type."

She gave me a smile that said I was being foolish again. "Are you really going to tell me that you felt nothing for Arthur that was a little different? That he didn't leave an impression that you can't shake. And not in a bad way."

The only response I gave her was a noncommittal shrug, but it didn't throw her off the scent.

She continued. "There is a palpable connection between you two. Same as the others you're about to go looking for. And the fact that it's directly influenced by his mortal enemies is an even bigger blow to Bel's ego."

"But I wouldn't—"

"Ultimately, you have no control over it. That's where that amulet comes in. They devoted themselves to the service of the Titans, and you were born of those same Titans. In a way the Desma are bound to serve you as well, but as that would be to the ultimate benefit of the creatures we're fighting against..."

"Can't utilize it. Right."

"Your biggest challenge is resisting that call you'll feel to them. Some part of you will always respond to the Desma. You'll feel safe and content. Maybe more than that." She shook her head. "You can't trust it."

I nodded, trying to ignore the gnawing ache in my heart. Even though my interaction with Arthur was brief, that rapturous kind of attraction would be easy to get used to. And the look of amazement and excitement in his eyes when he realized who I was...

"Let's head back. I really think you should find another one tonight, it might help you come to grips with all this. At the very least, you'll be able to do something and not just sit and brood," she teased.

I mocked her, parroting her words in a high-pitched voice. "That's what you sound like right now."

Risha laughed and got to her feet. After one last look at the deep shadows falling over the gully, I followed.

I barely spoke to Bel as I passed him, heading down to the basement. He gave me an "I'm sorry" glance but stayed out of my way. The warring sides of my mind played tug of war over whose side I should be on, but ultimately it wasn't much of a question.

Whichever side the Titans weren't on.

I may be pissed at Bel right now, but we were doing the right thing. Whether I would actually hand over any of the Desma again until I got assurances about their treatment remained to be seen. If this elite that I was about to go and find, that had already traced back the connection between us and knew I was out in the world somewhere, was more like the monster I expected, all the better. Arthur very likely could have been an anomaly or just a great scam artist.

Going through all the usual steps for tracking wasn't necessary this time, but I had no plans to tell Risha anything about the back trace that the Desma ran on me. He'd one-upped me at my own game.

Settling into my pillow cocoon, Risha left me to my own devices. I waited until I heard her disappear up the stairs and close the door. I stepped into the current of time that led to the place I'd tracked him and within the blink of an eye, I was standing in tall grass, the sky above me clear and blue. A layer of dew blanketed everything and mists rose from the ground.

A lake was alive with the shapes of ducks and swans just visible moving within the dense fog lying overtop it. Before I left, I'd grabbed the appropriate attire. Only problem was, it was more friendly if you were spending most of your time inside. The simple linen dress was perfect for the middle of summer in late Iron Age Briton. The time I'd landed in was decidedly not summer, late spring at most. The chill was seeping through me already. Amateur mistake, but all the more reason to make it quick.

On the other side of the lake, I could just make out the looming shapes of trees through the dense mist, their crowns bursting through the fog and reaching for the bright morning sun. I was on the edge of a vast forest. Movement caught my eye, a four-legged figure stalking the treeline, its solid black shape creeping closer to the shore. It drank before lifting its massive head and even through the gloom I could see its yellow eyes, glowing across the distance.

All at once a sensation of knowing rose within me and I gasped. That was him. The Desma.

It blinked and bared its teeth before moving back toward the trees. The fog closed up behind it, a solid wall of gray.

"Where are you going?" I mused. I opened my senses and cast out for him, confused as to why I couldn't feel him instinctively.

There was nothing, no response. It was like there was no Desma here at all, but I'd *just* seen him.

I took a seat on a large flat rock by the water, watching the fog burn away under the sun's rays, trying to figure out what was blocking me. Short of going into a trance, I tried everything I could think of.

Something was wrong. I decided to return to my time and rethink my approach, but when I reached for time...

Panic jolted through me. I couldn't feel it! No matter how many times I tried, I was shut out.

I was stuck here.

A howl went up from the woods nearby and I froze as that same feeling of knowing took me over again, accompanied by a small thrill as a thought echoed through my mind with the same resonance.

Mine.

He had me in his sights. Was this his doing? That shouldn't even be possible.

I fingered the amulet around my neck. Maybe this was backfiring? There wasn't any magick coming off it that I could sense, but I wasn't taking chances.

The clasp bent in my haste to remove it and I tossed it aside, reaching again for the time stream. I bit back a cry of frustration when my efforts amounted to nothing.

The howl faded and went unanswered. I watched the shadows within the trees for the wolf to reappear, but it stayed hidden. Invisible eyes bored into me while I groped around in the deep grass to find the amulet, my fingertips finally grazing it while I scanned for danger. It was icy cold when I slipped it back around my neck.

When I no longer felt like I was being watched , I set out.

I didn't know what I was looking for, but I was determined to keep moving until something felt right and my gut started talking to me again. Or until I ran into the wolf that howl belonged to. Whichever came first.

Unfortunately, it was neither. It was the rain that got me, and several run-ins with humans that made it clear anyone who seemed different was not welcome.

People in this time were far more sensitive to magick than the modern era, so keeping things on the DL, especially when you're not in a big city where it's easy to blend in among the crowds, was tough to say the least. I'd already met sheep shearers that threatened to cut my throat when they could sense I wasn't human. Women, cleaning clothing in a stream, cursed at me and began hurling rocks. I'd gotten as far away as I could before they could summon the menfolk.

I thought I might finally be in luck and find somewhere to call a home base for the time being when I'd wandered into a small village. I approached an elderly woman who had an air about her, maybe a Stranger or at least a wise woman that might be amenable to Strangers.

Nope. Not even a little. The woman had spit and cursed and almost stabbed me with a spindle.

So it had been a long night of shivering in the icy rain when, in the bleak dawn light, a small child with a basket of berries happened upon me in my poor excuse for a camp. I must've looked like a drowned rat.

I watched her with apprehension, but she showed no sign of being ready to fight me.

She wore a rough linen dress and cap to cover her thick curls, wiping at her face and smearing dirt on her cheek as she watched me with curious eyes. She held out the basket and offered me a berry. When she saw my hesitation, the girl took one and popped it into her mouth.

"They're not poison," she said with a giggle, before pushing the basket back toward me.

"Oh," I smiled. "Thank you."

The berry was sour as it burst on my tongue, but I resisted grimacing, nodding my thanks. The girl turned and nodded her head for me to follow.

We walked a short distance to a camp that blended in so well with its surroundings, I hadn't even noticed it was there. The kind of place you go to hide. The few people that were out and about acknowledged me and went back to their duties, showing no fear or an intent to attack.

And among them all, I could sense the powerful essence of Strangers.

The girl led me toward a larger hut at the end of the rows. A man stood guard outside the tent and eyed me with suspicion as we approached.

"I thought we told you to stop bringing home strays?" he growled. The girl was utterly unfazed by this large man many times her senior and stuck her tongue out at him.

"Welcome to the Vale," she said to me, before smiling and running off.

CHAPTER TWELVE

Meg

The guard gave me a long look before he stuck his head inside the curtain and spoke to someone. A deep male voice answered, and the warrior grunted in reply, pulling his head back and holding the curtain open for me to enter.

The warmth inside the hut was welcoming, a cheery, small fire blazing in the center of the room. What little smoke there was drifted through a hole in the roof. Around the fire were who appeared to be a chief and his wives. He was draped in furs and his beard was elaborately braided, studded with gems and gold. The women with him, three in total, were dressed similarly, but one woman with bright red hair had the most jewels and gold circling her neck, wrists, and head than the other two. She was also very pregnant and one of the other women showed signs of a bump as well.

The chief stared at me calmly and I could feel his power reach out toward me, trying to get a better sense of what I was. He frowned. That was the reaction people most often had. I was a one-of-a-kind and my signature wasn't like anything any Stranger would recognize.

"So what brings you to our camp?" he asked.

I appraised him, tilting my head. "Is that the question you really wanted to ask?"

The chief smirked and got heavily to his feet. "No. But it would be rather rude to ask such things so soon after meeting." He gestured to himself. "I am Abban, chief of this camp." He motioned to each wife in turn, in seeming order of seniority. "These are my wives, Orlaith, Damnat and Muirne."

I bowed my head. "Meg. Honored to meet you." I debated how I wanted to tell my story. "I found myself lost and unable to get home. I've been wandering, looking for somewhere to stay until I can figure things out." It was still the truth; I just stretched it like taffy.

"Not having much luck, I would imagine," Orlaith said, scowling. "These are dangerous times for all of us."

"I was getting that impression, yes. I was met with fear and anger everywhere I went. And someone usually tried to bring a pointy object into the equation."

As I was speaking this ancient dialect of Brittonic language, I noticed how much harder my tongue had to work around the words. Knowing how to speak every language that's ever been spoken doesn't prevent your mouth and throat from suffering around unfamiliar sounds.

The fire hissed and crackled as fat dripped off a roasting salmon and my stomach growled. Suddenly, the delectable smell was all I could focus on.

I grinned, sheepish, and put my hands on my stomach like that would quiet it. "Sorry."

"Of course, you must be hungry." Orlaith motioned to Muirne, who began to draw items from a small larder, organizing them on a simple wooden trencher and handing it to me.

"Please," said Orlaith, motioning at a cushion. "Have a seat and warm yourself while you eat."

"Thank you," I said, settling in by the warmth and tucking in to a kind of hard cheese that I wasn't familiar with but had an almost yeasty aftertaste, fresh bread, and a dried salmon jerky that I would dream about later, it was so good.

"You are of course welcome to stay with us as long as you need," Abban offered, sitting back down next to his wives. "As you've probably noticed, we're quite the collection of Strangers here."

"Dare I ask what happened?" No matter the answer, it would be tragic.

Damnat exhaled sadly. "Most of us came together because our families and homes were destroyed or scattered. There's so much animosity toward Strangers, driven largely by the new religion spreading through the lands. We were neighbors, and now..."

"I'm so sorry." My appetite fled, and I set down the piece of half-eaten bread.

The chief forced a smile as his first wife comforted the other. "We rely on power in numbers and staying on the move. Trying not to raise the ire of any humans in the area."

"If you pardon my asking, why don't you just return to the Strangefells?"

Muirne snorted a laugh but cast her eyes down when she received an admonishing look from Damnat.

"What Muirne was so rudely seeking to point out," said Orlaith, "is that the Strangefells isn't much more welcoming.

There are uprisings, civil wars. The Ætherim are making a mess of things again."

"And you'd rather take your chances with humans than a host of powerful Strangers," I said.

Abban bowed his head. "The choices aren't ideal, but we're trying to keep people as safe as we can. Give them a home when they have nowhere else to go."

An imposing figure appeared in the doorway, stooping to duck under the lintel. When he straightened my breath caught. He had to have been almost seven feet tall, the top of his head brushing the ceiling of the tent.

His swarthy skin was tanned and displayed prominent scars beneath the head-to-toe tattoos in blue-green ink, the patterns surprisingly intricate for the stick-and-poke technology of the time. His tartan, draped across his chest, revealed a large, jagged scar right near his heart.

His dark braided hair was bundled at his nape, and I glimpsed moss-green eyes that wouldn't quite meet my own, instead roaming over me in appraisal. There was something unreadable in his face, but I didn't get the chance to work it out before he turned to his chief. This was absolutely the man I'd spied when I'd gone searching.

"Issa detected human scent. We should prepare to move."

The chief pushed to his feet and followed the man out the door.

"Why don't I take you around and introduce you to the others? You can get settled in—well, at least get comfortable with the new arrangements." Orlaith corrected herself with a grimace as she gazed after her husband. She paused. "That is, if you plan to stay?"

I looked after the tartan-clad warrior, excitement stirring within me. I realized I was staring and glanced back at the women, blinking rapidly. Orlaith smiled knowingly. "That was Gareth, one of our warriors. A wolf shifter."

And there was the confirmation.

"He's very tall," I said lamely.

All three women laughed at my pathetic attempt to be nonchalant.

"He certainly is." Orlaith slipped her arm through mine. "Come, Meg. Let's take a walk."

For the next few days, we traveled, and I quickly made friends. I'd see Gareth from time to time in camp, but he mostly seemed to run at the perimeter, scouting ahead and reporting back, keeping an eye out for potential dangers. He wasn't alone in this duty but there were only three others that wore the tartans and had the iron warrior rings in their beards.

One of the girls acted out a very spirited pantomime of how the men got those rings as she told the story of slaying an enemy and gathering jewelry or the fallen warrior's own beard rings to forge into a new bauble that would be woven into the victor's beard as evidence of the enemies he'd slain.

Instead of eliciting fear at the ferocity of such a man, it only made me more curious.

In the evenings, when we would all eat together around the fire, I would catch Gareth watching me, his eyes gleaming in the firelight. Flashing yellow. He was indeed the person I was here to find and a gnawing sensation in the pit of my stomach kept growing.

Every time I tried to approach, he'd see me coming a mile away and disappear into the trees, shifting into his wolf form and bounding off. He had to realize who I was, so what game was he playing at? A sudden wash of dread cascaded over me. What if he knew what I'd done to Arthur? Maybe he was planning the best way to exact revenge. He knew my purpose was to capture him and he wasn't letting it happen, he was just waiting for the perfect opportunity to get to me that wouldn't raise questions.

My fourth morning in camp, as I was heading out with some of the other women to check traps they'd set in the river, my dress got caught in a tangle of blackthorn. By the time I'd freed myself they were almost out of sight. I hurried to catch up, taking a shortcut I found while checking the previous day's traps, turning around a large boulder and finding myself face to face with an angry wolf shifter.

"Gareth," I breathed, bracing myself under his glare. The urge to run plucked at me for a heartbeat or two, but it wasn't out of a desire to save myself. My knees shook; I wanted him to chase me.

Get a grip, idiot! Risha warned you this would happen. Don't fall for it.

I backed up a few paces, but my feet scrambled on a slick, mossy stone. I threw my arms out to catch myself, bracing for the sharp pain of rocks on my tailbone.

A strong hand wrapped around my upper arm and pulled me upright. That same fire that lit within me at Arthur's touch flared brightly once again and we both gasped.

His gaze was intense before, but it smoldered with barely concealed promise now. Gareth's pupils had dilated, and his nostrils flared. He released my arm but trailed his fingers downward, the tips of them brushing the back of my hand and leaving heat trails in their wake.

"Thank you." The words forced their way around my constricted throat, breaths coming in short pants. A flush rose to my cheeks under his intense scrutiny. The part of my brain that was able to focus on my real task fumbled for my amulet, but for the life of me, I couldn't remember how to activate it.

Gareth's fingertips grazed my cheek, and he growled low in his chest as I turned my head to rest it fully in his hand while simultaneously baring my throat to him.

In a flash of movement I was pinned to the boulder, his hands under my thighs as he held me there, the thin fabric of my dress shoved up around my hips. It had settled between my legs, making a thin, frustrating barrier as Gareth rolled his hips against me. He claimed my mouth with his own and I'd never felt such longing in a kiss. He wanted to devour me, make me his.

I ran my hands over his wide, muscular shoulders and wrapped my legs tight around him, moaning against his lips, wholly caught up in him. Until my friends began calling for me.

Gareth wrenched himself away and set me roughly on my feet before stalking into the trees. I stared after him, mouth agape, panting. This was starting to be a trend with the Six, getting fired up and walking away, leaving me wanting more.

As I rejoined my friends at the river, I realized I could feel Gareth out there in the woods. It seemed my ability to track the Desma was back. I reached out for the time stream and swore. Still nothing on that end. So, I was once again connected to my intended target, able to sense him every minute of the day, but I was stuck here with him. Great.

CHAPTER THIRTEEN

Gareth

As we sat around the fires that night, I watched Meg as she chatted and mended the holes the blackthorn had torn in her dress. The clearing emptied and the three women she was sitting with excused themselves to bed. We were the only ones left now.

I didn't quiet my steps as I crossed the short distance to her fire. She was just finishing up her mending and knew it was me without looking. "Can I help you with something?" she asked.

I resisted a smile at the needy tone in her voice, which became even more difficult when she wrinkled her nose, realizing how she sounded.

I dropped down next to her and made myself comfortable on one of the abandoned cushions. She continued mending, tying the loose end and biting off the remainder with her teeth.

"I'll leave you to your brooding then," she said, getting to her feet.

Just speak to her, man.

"Wait, Megiste. Please."

She froze. "I haven't told anyone my full name."

"I'm not just anyone." I patted the cushion she'd vacated. She stared at it blankly and chose to sit one cushion over instead. A smile flashed across my face. "I learned it when I connected to you, when you first began to look for me."

I picked up a stick and prodded at the logs in the fire, sparking up the embers. "I apologize. For earlier." When I completely lost all control the minute she'd bared her throat to me.

Meg stiffened, and a blush rose to her face, but she only shrugged.

"Why are you really here?" I asked.

I'd been going through the scenarios since she arrived. I'd felt her come through, her signature undeniable as the same one that I'd felt spying on me only hours earlier. When I'd traced that back to the source, I'd seen her briefly, knew her for what she was. For what she would be.

But she showed no sign that she was aware of her purpose. I'd had my doubts when she appeared in camp and her signature disappeared, but after our interlude in the woods it had returned stronger than before. And while she surely had identified me, her reaction was not what I would have expected.

She still hadn't answered, staring resolutely into the dying fire and seeming conflicted about how to answer. "There's no way this is a coincidence," I supplied. "The daughter of Kronos just happens upon my camp, clearly from another time. But you're not here for our bond."

Meg jerked and sat up straighter. "What is this bond?"

I sighed. That was a big question with a complicated answer.

She made to stand up again, impatient. I held up my hand.

"There were six of us. The most trusted advisors and generals among the Titans' armies. We fought side by side with them, to secure the future against the Ætherim, who were being driven mad by the power they wielded over mortals and Strangers alike."

She rolled her eyes, and I frowned. "Something the matter?" I asked sternly.

"I've heard every possible iteration of this story you can imagine. The Titans were heroes, the Ætherim were the enemy of all. I am from another time, you're right about that. From far in the future, in fact. The Ætherim aren't evil dictators. They stay out of the politics of the Strangefells and human world, for the most part."

I leaned back and squared my shoulders. "I'm sure it appears like that, but how do you know for sure? How do you know they aren't showing you what you want to see?"

"The same could be said for your argument."

I tilted my head in acknowledgment. "True. How much can any of us know about the intentions of such powerful beings? All I know is what I've seen firsthand."

"Same."

I appraised her and asked quietly, "Are the Ætherim the ones that sent you here?"

Meg squirmed in her seat, and I heard her pulse jump. "Why would they do that?"

"A good question. One might think they were planning something that isn't going to end well for myself or the others. And you're fully onboard with helping them do it."

Her face flushed red again, and she worried her bottom lip with her teeth. I stared, wanting very much to claim it with my own teeth... before moving on to other, more sensitive, areas.

"And I might also think that you'd be quite conflicted, considering what we obviously feel toward each other."

She drew up, indignant. "You mean the cheap ploy where you attempt to manipulate me with sex to win me over to your side?"

I frowned in confusion. "Is that what you think this is? A trick?"

Her certainty faltered before she gathered it back up around her like armor. "Of course it is. Why else would I fall all over you without even knowing you?"

I schooled my expression and told her the truth. With grave sincerity, I said, "My natural magnetism, of course."

The retort she'd had ready died on her tongue and a burst of laughter came out instead. She was even more beautiful when she laughed. I moved over to the cushion next to her, not wanting to risk being overheard. The people here were my family, but they weren't aware of who I really was or what was hiding in my history.

"When the war turned against the Titans and we knew that victory was no longer possible, myself and the others were flung off into different time periods. All in the past, never forward. Do you know why?"

She shook her head slowly.

"They didn't know what the future would look like after they lost. They weren't sure the Ætherim could be trusted with it, positive that their power-hungry nature would destroy everything before too long."

Before she could reply, I pushed ahead. "There was a plan in place a few months before everything fell apart. The Titans used the last of their power to secret the six of us away in time so we would be able to protect their last hope when it came along."

That cold cynicism settled back over her. "Their last hope? You mean me?" Her voice was flat, emotionless. Ready for the next pile of bullshit she expected me to shovel at her. How could I help her see the truth?

"You may not believe it, but yes. None of us were sure what form you would take, even the Titans. But the spirit you possess is the same bright energy of your father and the rest of your family. It's unmistakable."

"Stop calling him my father like I was born a natural child. I'm a construct, formed of the bits of energy he could spare."

My brow furrowed, and I shook my head. "You may be a construct, but you weren't an afterthought composed of spare parts. All of the Titans contributed to your making, giving you the best pieces of themselves."

She narrowed her eyes and I could see her mind churning over the information. "Even if that's the case—"

"It is."

"It doesn't change the fact that I was supposed to be a mindless vessel existing only to break them out of jail." She scoffed. "You know, that's real rich. The Titans acting like the Ætherim were the ones that were power hungry. The Ætherim had no choice but to fight." Her voice steadily rose in volume and her cheeks burned with anger. "The Titans wanted a war, and they gave it to them. How can you defend them? They were no better than the Ancients."

I recoiled, and my gaze was hard as I stared at her. She met my glare, refusing to back down.

"Meg, your family—"

"They're not my family," she growled.

"Your family," I began again, "were entreating to be left alone. The pantheons were forming, sides were being chosen, and they wanted to be left out of it. When the Ætherim pushed, the Titans pushed back. And when the Ætherim fell victim to the power they wielded over the mortals, the Titans wanted none of it. Many of them had a soft spot for mortals. Prometheus just wanted to give them a fighting chance and look at what the Ætherim did to him."

Her expression changed, and she sat back. "Wow."

When she didn't say anything else, I nodded, cautiously optimistic that she'd heard me.

"You're delusional."

My face fell, but I forged ahead, regardless. "Kronos was your chief creator, so you'd have a powerful gift of manipulating time. So you could find us. The Titans assured us that if nothing else went to plan, the fact that you'd be driven to seek us out would remain, no matter what."

She crossed her arms tightly in front of her. "Doesn't it defeat the purpose of making people my guardians if they aren't even in the same time period as me?"

"It may not have been ideal, but it was the only option. The Titans knew it would have to be a journey on your part because they wouldn't have enough power to bring us to you when the time came. But once we were all united, we'd be an unstoppable force."

"To break them out of prison!" She leaped to her feet. "It all boils down to that! We're supposed to free them and just watch them wreak havoc trying to tear down the Ætherim and everything and anyone else that gets in their way!"

I stared, aghast, at this woman who I'd thought would be the catalyst that would change everything. She would reunite me with my brothers-in-arms, and we'd once again be fighting alongside the Titans to fulfill our purpose and win our glory.

My emotions vacillated between anger and disappointment, settling on fury toward whoever had poisoned her mind. "Who got to you? Who made you so unable to listen to reason? Made you hate us with such intensity?"

"An Ætherim. I don't know how much I even trust him right now, but it's still more than you. And the minute I'm able, I'm sending you back to my time to meet him. He'll decide what to do with you."

So that was it, then. I got to my feet and walked off into the darkness.

Chapter Fourteen

Meg

A flash of yellow eyes, tinted with betrayal and hurt, and they blinked away. A second later I heard a mournful howl and four legs running swiftly to a destination unknown.

The next morning broke chilly and gray, a glistening mist lying over the valley in which we'd set camp. There was an uneasy quiet in the dawn, holding its breath in anticipation of something.

I spent the night staring at the ceiling of my tent, the gentle snores of the women I was bunking with unable to lull me to sleep like they usually did. I'd been too harsh. I shouldn't have lost my temper; we were both being played by forces bigger than us.

With a sigh, I gave up and decided to do some early morning foraging, maybe find a few extras for everyone's breakfast. The dew soaked through my slippers immediately as I crossed the short way to the woods. The air within the forest was heavy with an invasive presence but I shook it off.

It amazed me how easily these people had accepted me into their fold. It would be hard to leave them once I could access time again. Maybe I could come back once the job was finished, but they probably wouldn't want me around after I spirited away one of their protectors.

My breath caught in my throat at the pang of guilt that hit me right in the gut. These were the kind of people that would trounce bad vibes out of here immediately. Would Gareth be able to fool them all like that?

A large crack echoed in the dense woodland, and I froze, listening for any footsteps to go with it. When everything remained peaceful, I moved to the patch of wild garlic in the clearing ahead, already anticipating the excitement on Rowan's face when she got to add the fragrant herb to her porridge. I was so focused on my goal I didn't notice I wasn't alone until a hand snaked from behind a tree and wrapped around my mouth.

I was yanked backward with a strangled cry.

"Quiet now, Meg. It's important."

Heart still in my throat, I nodded. There was an urgency in Gareth's voice that overwrote any desire I had to elbow him in the gut. He released me and I turned. He pointed a few feet away, a grieved look on his face as he stared at a shape on the ground.

It was a massive wolf with silver fur. A thick arrow shaft had pierced his back and run straight through his heart, the bright, silver-coated tip thrusting out the front of his chest.

"Issa?" I choked. A couple of stumbling footsteps and I was crouching next to him, resting a hand on his shoulder. I looked back at Gareth, staring mournfully at his fallen brother, pain etched into his features.

"What happened?"

"I—"

A horn sounded out of the gloom, ringing clearly through the woods and Gareth turned sharply, a snarl ripping from his throat. He pelted toward the field, and I took off after him. When he realized I was behind him, he stopped so suddenly I almost ran into him.

"Go hide," he growled. I put my hands up, not arguing, and he continued racing back to camp.

I had no intention of following his order.

When enough distance was between us, I bolted through the trees, quickening my pace when the screams and sounds of battle broke the silence.

Stopping just short of the open field, I stared in horror. Men were surging out of the woods on the opposite side of the field, surrounding the entire camp. I could already smell the blood in the air, the copper tang settling on my tongue. I ducked an errant blast of magick and a wash of splinters fell over me as the trunk of the tree behind me shattered.

Two wolves tore through the human horde, attacking the perimeter at the weak points and scattering the densely packed attackers. They worked in tandem to drive the horde into groups, making a gap for people to escape through. The only other shifters in the group were small animals and none of the magi were adept enough to use their skills for battle, so they ran.

As the first of my friends cleared the trees, I grabbed the biggest fallen log I could comfortably wield and took a batter's stance.

I heard a yelp and saw Burdock, a russet-colored wolf, had collapsed and was being set upon by humans, silver blades catching the rising sun. I didn't see Gareth anywhere and despite my efforts, my gorge rose.

The first of the humans reached the trees, and I swung, connecting with his head and knocking him out. Another couple of swings and he wasn't going after any of my friends again.

A fog built and roiled around us as I took another attacker to the ground, so thick I could barely see my hand in front of my face.

The attackers called to each other and shouted jeers and taunts to their Stranger prey. Screams punctuated the fog only to be cut short, followed by a horrible silence. Breeze buffeted the vapor in swirls, making eerie shadows in the carnage. Shapes bearing swords, spears, and axes moved through the mist, slowly searching. I liberated the axe off the man I'd just taken down and moved between the trees, head on a swivel.

It was heavy in my hands, and I hoped once the time came to use it, the action would be instinctual. The leather grip on the handle was rough, making it easier to keep hold of despite the sweat slicking my palms. I tried to calm the shaking in my body as I moved forward, the adrenaline overloading my system.

I was going hunting.

A bellow of a war cry was my only warning before an axe whipped toward my head. I flattened myself against a tree, closing my eyes as the air current gusted against my face a hairsbreadth from striking me. The axeman took another swing, building on the momentum of the last, and I ducked as the cold edge of the weapon sank deep into a thick trunk.

While he was struggling to free the axe, I ran headlong into a wall of mist. It rose around me, concealing me from pursuit but blinding me at the same time. I held my arms ahead of me, so I didn't run into a tree.

A thick forearm surged out of the mist to grab at me, snagging my dress and yanking me back. A face smeared with ichor and bearing a cruel smile loomed out of the fog, the fierce eyes of the warrior shining with the insanity of blood lust as they appraised me.

His shoulders were corded with muscle, and he bore several weapons strapped to his torso. His beard hung thick with iron rings and the madness in his eyes said he'd chosen his next victim.

His lip curled back in a sneer, and he threw me to the ground, lifting his axe over his head. Suddenly his back arched, and he howled in pain, spinning to confront another attacker and revealing long claw marks down his back.

I scrambled to my feet, drawn by the terrified screams of a woman and child. I hefted the axe and lurched forward, the mist parting to reveal a single fighter standing over the fallen body of a man. Drake.

Panic clawed at me as the attacker raised his sword and turned to Rowan as she clung helplessly to her son, tears cascading down her cheeks as she stared in horror at her dead husband.

My feet moved, silent, as I charged the warrior, only making a sound right before I buried the axe in his back, causing his strike to miss Rowan and her son by inches.

The brute fell to the side and Rowan sobbed. "Thank you."

Rowan's son couldn't tear his eyes away from his father as the man stared at the sky with unseeing eyes. Rowan scooped him into her arms and buried his face in her shoulder.

"I'm so sorry," I said, scanning for anything that could be used as cover. "You've got to find a place to hide." My gaze lit on two large, flat stones that had collapsed into each other. I grabbed her hand and pulled her along. "Here."

The two barely fit in the small space. Once they were secure, I began to tear up the long grass and gather fallen branches, stacking them up as naturally as possible around the stones to conceal mother and son.

Rowan grabbed my hand. "Be safe."

Her fingers were cold as they gripped mine and I nodded. "You too."

I couldn't stop the tears as I piled on the last of the grasses, not knowing if I'd ever see her again.

With one last look to make sure they were concealed, I darted off, hoping the ploy would be enough to save them. I stalked over to the human I'd slain and wrenched the axe from his back. The only thing I wanted in that moment was revenge. This carnage would not go unanswered.

Another mortal was stalking cautiously forward about thirty yards away, still blinded by mist, spear at the ready. This one was wearing thick leather armor. I backed away as he drew near, stepping carefully on the bramble underfoot and flattening myself against a tree as I waited for his approach. Blood added to the sheen of sweat on my hands and made my grip on the axe slip as I adjusted my hold for a better swing.

His muffled footsteps on the thick, leafy carpet were only a few feet away. The spearpoint appeared in my peripheral and as soon as the man's arm was within view, I raised the axe and brought it down. It sank deeply into the bone, and stuck. The man howled, dropping his spear and falling back, almost taking me with him, but I held my footing and gripped the axe tighter as it squelched free of his flesh.

I barely heard the second attacker running toward us, drawn by his comrade's pained wail. His cry of outrage as he barreled down on us had me whirling just in time.

I ducked and leaned back to avoid his sword strikes, but he kept coming, fierce and fast. I dodged and winced as my elbow struck a boulder. My fingers went numb, and the axe slipped from my hands. He swung and just barely missed my throat.

I backpedaled and tripped, sprawling facedown and eating a mouthful of dirt. Still spitting and spluttering, my hand found the shaft of the spear the first warrior had dropped and I raised it in a blind defense.

His forward lunge landed him on the spearpoint, the blade sinking deep into his gut and bringing him to a stuttering halt. Blood gushed from his mouth and spattered all over my chest and face. I flopped onto my back to get better leverage and twisted the spear, sending the man's body sprawling off to the side.

Blood was rushing in my ears and my vision tunneled on the fallen warrior, not yet having succumbed to blood loss from the arm wound I'd dealt him. Fury and madness took over, bloodlust singing through me with a jarring electric sensation. I retrieved the axe and advanced. He tried to scurry back, but I stomped a foot on his chest, brought the axe up and swung it in a clean arc. Red droplets sprayed in a fine mist on my face as the man's head was cleanly severed and rolled a few feet away before settling in the roots of a tree.

My breath was labored, coming in heaving gasps as I fought to tame the overwhelming urge to tackle and kill every enemy warrior I saw. They still had height and strength to their advantage, not to mention superior numbers. Running headlong into the fray would only get me killed.

Ahead, I spotted three humans fanning out and weighed my options, separating them seeming like the best choice. I tracked the men as I moved around them, never taking my eyes off them for a second.

When I backed into something too soft to be a tree and too hard to be anything but a muscle-bound, tattooed, tartan-wearing warrior, my heart leaped to my throat. As I turned, Gareth's eyes pinned me to the spot, the rise and fall of his chest beneath his tartan calm and steady.

Chapter Fifteen

Meg

The tattoos that ran up and down his arms seemed to be alive as they glistened with perspiration and blood, many wounds already healing, but the most garish of them still bled freely.

"You're okay," I breathed, both relieved and conflicted; I wasn't getting out of the choice I'd have to make.

His eyes flicked behind me, and he seized my arm, dragging me behind him while simultaneously bringing his hand up to deflect the weapon hurtling at us. The spear thwacked into a tree and stuck fast, the crack acting like a starting shot that launched Gareth at the attackers.

He ran straight for the fool who launched the spear and was watching Gareth in sick fascination, barely lifting his axe in time to block the claws that had erupted from Gareth's fingers.

With a howl, Gareth knocked the axe from his opponent's hand and drove his claws deep into the man's chest, gurgles erupting from the attacker's throat before he slumped over.

The other two were running at Gareth, weapons at the ready. Gareth threw an axe overhand, and it buried itself into one of their chests. The final man standing was outmatched against the wolf. He tried to defend himself while falling back toward the field where his fellows would have a hope of coming to his aid.

Gareth didn't let him get that far.

His other form was taking over now, and I watched as Gareth became half wolf, half man in a grotesque tableau from a D-list horror film. I could smell the distinct odor of the human shitting himself as he fell to his knees before the raging beast and begged for his life.

Gareth ended him with a mighty swipe of his claws, and once again, silence fell.

There was no more fighting or distant screams. Only the groans of dying and a fetid smell of emptied bowels and spilled guts filled the air.

"Rowan!" I exclaimed, running full out back to the spot where I'd hidden her.

"Meg!" Gareth called. I could hear his heavy footfalls behind me. He may have a bigger stride, but I was faster and raced ahead—stopping short when I saw the scattered grasses and the empty hiding place. And the blood that smeared the rocks.

"No!" I screamed, pelting into the clearing to search for Rowan.

Strong arms gripped me like a vise and hauled me off my feet. I landed heavily on Gareth's shoulder as he carried me away from the massacre.

I beat at his back, clawed at anything I could reach, but he didn't slow. "Put me down! There might be survivors, we have to find them!" I aimed a fist at his kidney and that earned a grunt of pain from him, but he still carried me on.

"Gareth, please!" I begged. "I have to know!"

He dumped me on my feet and gripped my shoulders so fast my head was still spinning when he peered into my face. He waited until I was focused on him before he spoke. "Meg." Shock radiated off him and his voice hitched. "There's no one left. You don't want to see them that way."

I stared back over his shoulder. He'd already covered quite the distance and the most telltale feature of where camp had been was the smoke from the fires rising into the sky.

"More will come. We have to move."

Tears filled my eyes. "Why did they do that?" I asked, shellshocked. "Why did they attack?"

"For no other reason than they were cowards."

"It was mostly women and children!" Hysteria tinged my voice. I'd seen many awful things, but never carnage like this. He needed to make it make sense. "They were innocent!" I screamed.

Gareth pulled me in and crushed me to his chest and I sobbed, gripping onto him like the only lifeline I had. Although, at that moment, that's exactly what he was. All thoughts of him being the enemy vanished. There was a very real, tangible enemy that had come for the people we both cared about.

He held me while I cried and even after the tears let up, his arms remained tight around me. Only when I started to push away did he release me. I couldn't stop my mouth from parting in surprise to see the tear stains that ran through the blood and dirt on his own face.

"I have a camp about a day's walk from here. Will you come with me?"

"Even after I threatened to send you to your capture or death?" I asked. "You don't owe me anything."

Gareth huffed a breath and managed a small smile. "A little trouble adjusting is to be expected." He raised a hand, wiping smears of blood from my face with gentle strokes. "And I will protect you until the very second I'm taken from you."

Read: me sending him away, I thought, guilt creeping up my chest.

"You may have made an oath to the Titans, but I'm not holding you to anything," I tried again, hoping to dissuade him.

"You're not getting rid of me that easily."

"That's not what I'm doing. I'm offering to let you go on your way, without interfering even more than I already have."

Gareth looked away from me and busied himself with cleaning blood off his hands. The brittle scratching of dry grass as he attacked his cuticles was grating. "There's nothing left here for me. My pack disbanded and I'd been alone for a good many years before joining the caravan. They were my family, in all the ways that mattered. The chief was a great man."

The ache in my heart split open again and fresh pain rose for the loss. If I felt it this keenly, I could only imagine how bad it was for Gareth.

"There's only one way to go." His eyes met mine. "Regardless of what happened in that clearing, my place is with you."

"I don't think you know what you're asking. I can't just walk away from Bel and the mission."

Gareth's eyes narrowed at the mention of Bel's name, but he didn't explode with anger like Arthur had. I continued. "I'm still not sure what's going on, or who to trust, but my goal to keep the Titans locked away hasn't changed. The only thing I'm decently positive about is that I won't be sending you back to my time."

"Then how will you accomplish your goal?" he asked, refocusing on scrubbing his hands.

"I'll find another way."

Gareth nodded and dropped his makeshift nail brush, brushing the remnants of dried grass off his hands. "Let's keep moving."

I fell into step beside him, aware of how much he had to shorten his strides to make that possible.

We walked along until we came to a stream, running beautifully clear and sparkling in the sunlight.

"Is it safe to drink?" I asked him.

He nodded, scanning the surrounding area. His nostrils dilated as he scented the air.

"Anything we should be worried about?"

"No, not yet anyway."

I crouched and cupped my hands in the water, drinking deeply. It was cold and fresh, and I felt a little more like myself again.

I splashed my face and attempted to scrub as much blood off as I could, and Gareth knelt next to me and did the same.

The valley we were in was lovely and peaceful. A world away from what we'd just run from. I stared into the distance, the gentle rushing of water soothing me and lulling me into deep thought.

"Are you ready to go?"

Gareth's voice jarred me from my self-induced hypnosis. I hummed in agreement, and we continued on.

We tried to make light conversation, avoiding anything about what had happened in the clearing, but it weighed heavily, the unspeakable nature of it waiting to rear up and clobber us the moment we gave it a chance.

Just around nightfall, I saw a small camp up ahead. As we approached, Gareth started to gather kindling and piled it in a fire pit that held the remnants of previous fires. The ashes looked like they'd been there a while.

"Was this another regular camping spot for—?" I couldn't bring myself to name them.

He shook his head and took out some flint, and we stared at the pile of kindling until the fire sparked to life. "This camp was only made for one."

My next question hit right at the center of the subject we'd mutually agreed to avoid. "Were you prepared for the attack to happen?"

He didn't immediately answer, busying himself with adding dry grass on the sparks to feed it, and I watched, mesmerized, as the flames began to chew through the fuel. The sticks weren't as dry as they could've been, so they took a moment to catch. The hiss and pop of the wood was comforting, as was the smell of burning pine that quickly began to permeate the space.

"No. I have several camps spread around that I used before I joined the caravan. My pack disintegrated and I became a lone wolf, unwillingly." He smiled sadly. "I'm not cut out for it."

Gareth got to his feet and moved to a tree, stretching his arm into a hollow and pulling out something wrapped in oilskin, followed by another, bigger bundle. The large one he tossed on the ground and the smaller he began to unwrap. He handed me a strip of dried meat before reaching into the pack he'd grabbed before we'd run from camp, revealing a fresh loaf of bread and a hunk of cheese.

I sniffed tentatively at the jerky, trying to discern what kind of protein it was.

"What, you don't like human meat?"

I balked and thrust the dried flesh away from my face. A roaring laugh from the other side of the fire filled the small camp, and I scowled at the wolf. "You've got a very dark sense of humor."

"Who said I was joking? I just thought your reaction was hilarious."

I threw the piece of jerky at him, horrified. His laughter redoubled as he caught it and took a huge bite, chewing and swallowing, before putting me out of my misery. "Alright, I was joking." He tossed me another strip. "Promise. It's bear."

That would explain the slightly rancid, oiliness of the meat. I nibbled a tiny bite off the end and tried not to grimace at the flavor. It must be an acquired taste. I handed the jerky back to Gareth, instead of throwing it this time. "I'll pass, but thank you."

He shrugged, continuing to devour his bear jerky and tearing a chunk of bread off instead, offering it to me. "You've got to eat something."

I gratefully took the bread and inhaled the aroma before taking a bite. Trying not to think about who had made the sourdough early this morning.

Gareth motioned to the hunk of cheese and pulled a skin of some kind of liquid out of his pack before taking a swig. "Help yourself." He offered me the skin. "It's mead. Pretty strong, so take it easy." He grinned. "If you start to get handsy I'm not going to stop you."

I almost took that as a challenge, but decided not to press my luck. I sipped the mead, and he was correct. It was stronger than any you were likely to find on liquor store shelves.

Before long the nocturnal critters were out and making a whole different cacophony of noise. A vixen shrieked in the distance, and I shuddered. Even knowing what made the sound, it was still awful to hear. The fire was burning low and Gareth added a couple of smaller logs to it, lost in his own thoughts. He stretched out on his side and rested his head in his hand.

"Tell me more about them."

He looked over at me. "The Titans?"

I chewed my lip but nodded. I should at least get more information, right?

Gareth sat up and moved a little closer. I was keenly aware of the heat of his body, and he was still a good three feet away.

"What do you want to know?"

Chapter Sixteen

Bel

"She should have been back by now." I'd paced this line through the basement so many times I'd lost track. "It's been three days. Did something happen to her?"

Risha tried to soothe me with her rational thinking. "You'd know if she was dead. Has her signature disappeared?"

"Almost, but no," I said. "But that doesn't change the fact that she should've been back. No matter how long it takes, she always returns—"

"—by the next day," Ursal finished. Carefully, he added, "We know."

"So give me another explanation," I snapped.

Risha shared a brief glance with her brother but looked away when I tried to catch her gaze. "What?" I looked between them. "For the god's sake, just say it!"

Ursal grit his teeth. "If she isn't back by now, there's a decent chance it's because she's not planning to come back."

I snarled and grabbed his throat, barely feeling his fingers scratching at the back of my hand as he choked.

"My lord, please!" Risha begged, moving next to her brother, hands hovering with the desire to help him but not daring to intervene. "You have to admit he's got a point."

My breath rattled in my chest as I exhaled heavily, slowly setting him down and releasing my grip on his neck one finger at a time.

"So what do we do?"

Risha was fussing over Ursal and not paying attention to me. "What do we do, Risha?" I snapped.

She leaped away from her brother with a start before she collected herself enough to return to her desk and start searching through books. "If—if she's not back in our time then I'm not sure there's anything we can do."

"Not good enough!" I slammed my hand on her desk, and she jumped before her shoulders hunched in protectively.

"Oh, don't go fetal on me, Risha," I sneered. "You've got too much work to do for me to risk having to replace you."

"My lord." Ursal's voice was rough, and he continued to massage his throat. I stared at him coldly, inviting him to continue. "Is there a chance that the Desma could've seduced her away?"

My lip curled in disgust. "I wouldn't think she was that weak. I drilled enough hatred of the Titans into her to overcome anything."

Risha made a noise, and I rounded on her, but she covered it with a cough.

I sniffed. "Fine. Keep looking for ways that we can circumvent the situation if needed and bring her back. I have a trip to make."

I opened my eyes to a familiar landscape that made my skin crawl. The air shimmered with heat and the acrid scent of sulfur burned my nose.

I cursed and brushed at my shirt sleeve where ash had already begun to settle. "Blasted Tartarus."

A hiss slithered down from somewhere high above me and I craned my head into the shadows, seeing a shape move within it. The faintest lines of fire ignited to form a pattern, a brightening outline of scales on a very large dragon.

As I watched, a giant pair of wings unfurled with a shower of sparks and a long sinewy neck stretched out from its place tucked into the creature's body. A reptilian face with a narrow snout and massive jaws fixed me with a toothy smile.

The dragon roared and a strong wind gusted through the cavern as it dropped from the ceiling and pumped its wings to settle on the ground, ropes of fiery spittle oozing from its mouth.

"Calm down, it's only me."

A ferocious hiss escaped past the jagged teeth, a forked tongue tasting the air.

"Been bored, have we?" I asked the sentinel. "Do I need to switch up the guards and put your hydra brethren on these gates instead?"

The dragon snarled and shook its head, sending sparks and globs of liquid fire everywhere. I wiped my face, disgusted, the burns minutely stinging as they healed. "Just step aside, idiot."

It lumbered out of the way with a grumble, the fire extinguishing from its throat. As I walked toward the gates of

Tartarus, I let my human guise drop. The world seemed so much smaller in my natural form, the giant portal ahead of me now perfectly fitting.

My senses were much sharper when I was fully manifested. I could hear every drip of water from the stalactites extending down from the ceiling, the humidity clinging and condensing in the—no pun intended—hellishly hot air. The sulfurous reek was burning my nose, and the ash left an acrid taste on my tongue.

The iron gates smelled of raw minerals and the flesh and blood that infused their parts, using the Titans' own magick against them. There were many more Titans before the wars than the ones remaining. These were the ones that opted to surrender instead of insisting on going down swinging like the others.

When I had these gates built, I'd used the broken bodies of the fallen, infused their bones into the bars, the muscle and sinew in the chains and bathed the whole thing in every drop of blood I could wring out of them. I wrapped them in so much magick and darkness and pain, even touching it would kill a Titan on the spot.

But not me. I set my hand to the doors and the chain slithered away, tucking into an alcove. The gates groaned and shuddered before they cracked open a fraction. I pushed firmly and they gave, swinging open with a long whine.

A smell like an abattoir hit me as soon as I crossed the threshold. Zader must've been in the middle of a fresh round of torture.

The gloom outside the gate was replaced with sunlight, lively green flora, beautiful trees and birdsong. If you could only block out the smells, you would think you were in a lovely park in the summertime. I smirked to myself. That had been a stroke of genius on my part, really. Make them stare at a world they couldn't have day in and day out. Let them be reminded of the lush paradise they fought so hard for while they were being eternally tortured.

I strode forward, my bare feet enjoying the feel of the thick grass between my toes.

There was a small rise preventing those entering the gates from seeing into the space beyond, but once that was cleared...

I took in a deep breath and a smile spread wide across my face. It was glorious.

Twelve Titans. Twelve individual tortures that would hurt them most, all stretched out below me with endless possibilities.

The warden for this prison was an old ally that fought by my side every step of the way during the wars. Zader was the most bloodthirsty creature I'd ever met. The perfect choice for the job.

A bellowed scream of pain echoed through the space but none of the other Titans made a sound. In the beginning, they'd howled and protested and shouted words of strength to whichever compatriot was being hosted in the special dungeon. But now they were silent. Perhaps I was finally wearing them down after so many thousands of years.

I passed by Helios and Atlas first.

Helios, always so proud of his chariot as he drove the sun across the sky, was now lying in a cube of convex glass, the very sun that was his identity, weaponized against him. He was almost through a whole cycle of being burned and roasted. He would get a day of reprieve in complete darkness and then the whole cycle started over.

Atlas was slowly being crushed. A chuckle escaped me. I'd been particularly clever with this one. The object of his torture was the collective weight of mankind's hubris. Every time they put themselves above everything else, the weight crushing him only got heavier. Which, since the Strangefells was now back in the mortal diaspora and modern mortals were the most close-minded—well, the weight was significant. The more it crushed him, the more he would be aware of how things were shaking out in the human world he'd pledged himself to defend.

Their eyes tracked me even as their ruined bodies stayed immobile, pure hatred in their glares. I continued past them and came to an expanse of verdant green, the lushest section here. A quick scan of the mound in the middle discerned familiar shapes.

"Rhea. What a beautiful garden you've grown."

Rhea could only look at me from a single good eye. The rest of her body was being consumed by the plants and insects sprouting from it. A tree had taken up residence in most of her body cavity, the root systems buried deep within her organs. One of those roots had traveled up her throat and out her eye socket. Rhea's was the slowest process of all of them, her torture cycles taking a couple hundred years before they started to repeat.

Another scream, guttural and wild, bounced off the walls. The door to Zader's chamber of horrors was up ahead. I only passed by one more Titan on my way.

Oceanus was lying in the middle of a sun-drenched patch of desert. There wasn't a drop of water to be had for him or the surrounding land. Harsh winds kicked up sandstorms that raked his desiccated skin. He was about halfway through his cycle, still a decent amount of hydration left in his muscle mass.

But everything else had collapsed and withered, his stomach just a hollow pit.

I entered the dungeon proper and saw that Zader had Pallas on the rack, taking him apart slowly with a dull knife.

"You haven't lost your touch. How long has it been?" I asked my chief torturer with a smile.

"I believe you mentioned something about a world war ramping up?" said Zader drolly. "What brings you here, my lord? Nothing serious I hope?"

My eyes narrowed at Pallas. "I have questions that need answering. About Megiste." I watched Pallas go still at the mention of her name, but he said nothing.

"The construct?" asked Zader.

"Yes, the very one. She's causing trouble. Got a little out of my control."

Zader hummed thoughtfully but simply carried on dissecting Pallas, the latter's grin at the mention of their "hope" being out of my control wiped away in an instant. All the tools that Zader had at his disposal were specially designed to make the Titans feel pain. Conventional methods wouldn't have done more than cause a nuisance.

I clapped Zader on the shoulder. "I suppose I'll leave you to it. Enjoy yourself."

"Always, my lord."

I walked back out of the chamber. I wouldn't get much out of them, but I could at least read their expressions. If I was going to discover what I needed from anyone, it would be Kronos himself.

His torture was in the center of it all, so they could all watch their king brought low.

I began to climb the hill, and the smell hit me first thing. At the crest, I was greeted with the mighty leader on his hands and knees, covered in filth, crawling across the shattered shards of the crowns of all the kings in the earthly realm and Strangefells that had followed him into battle.

He'd been castrated as well. Just the final coup de gras, really.

"Kronos, old friend." I took a seat on the bench I'd added so I could relax and observe my handiwork. "Been up to anything interesting?"

Kronos said nothing, only continued to crawl as he was compelled to. I raised my hand, and he stilled. "Go ahead. Stand up, stretch your legs a bit. It's been a hundred years since you've had the chance."

The Titan only sat back on his heels and watched me.

I clucked my tongue. "So disobedient, so defiant. Just like your daughter."

His eyes sharpened and a shaky breath shuddered in his chest.

"Well"—I gestured to his ruined genitals—"not a real one of course." I smiled.

"She's been helping me on my mission to snap up all the links that can be traced back to you. That might hold any power that could aid you in escaping, any kind of anchor tethering you to the other realms."

I got a growl in response this time. "Yes. I have her convinced that you are the root of all evils. Or at least I did. Your elite are proving somewhat of a bother."

Kronos grinned, and his nostrils flared. Vocal cords that hadn't been used in centuries for anything other than screaming, wheezed as they came to life. "Those bonds are stronger than any power you'll ever have over her. She'll find her way back to her purpose."

I rolled my eyes and waved my hand dismissively. "Spare me the sage words and idle threats. She's already sent one of them to me. Arthur?"

The slightest tick in Kronos's left eye betrayed his feelings on the matter.

"She served him up on a platter for me to toy with and kill at my leisure. You really did make a mess of things. It wasn't hard to make her hate you. Those Ætherim allies you sent her to live with were real pieces of work. Of course, even if you did manage to get free, they certainly won't be around to receive the rewards they were counting on. Did you know they kept her locked away, treating her like their golden goose? Relaying tales of your savagery and awesome power. Everything you'd tear down and remake when you were free? They did most of my work for me and they weren't even aware."

Something softer appeared in his glare; guilt.

"You didn't realize. Interesting. I guess there were many mistakes made when you rushed those plans through in the last days before the war ended, hmm? It took you a couple thousand years longer than you thought it would to create your secret weapon"—I grinned and leaned in toward him—"which I knew about the whole time, by the way, and then when you finally managed it, you screwed it up even further by handing a fresh construct to a bunch of power-hungry Ætherim. They may have been allies, but they're still Ætherim. Their own habits will win out, always."

"Did they hurt her?" he asked sharply.

"Only with social isolation and neglect at first. But later on, when the magick went further awry and she started developing a mind of her own, they resorted to beatings to bring her back in line."

Kronos growled and his fists clenched.

"Oh, my." I placed my fingertips against my chest in mock amazement. "Don't tell me you actually care for the girl?" New ideas were coming to me. "Maybe, when this is all over, instead of killing her outright, I'll bring her down here. She can join you all." I stood, already imagining the punishments.

"How many elites are there?" I asked offhand, facing away from him.

From the corner of my eye I could see him staring off into space, considering all the things I'd already told him, all the road blocks I'd put in his way. The plans I'd ruined before they even got off the ground. "Six."

I spun around, triumphant, and his eyes widened as he realized his mistake.

"Thank you, old friend. Our journey together will be at an end soon." I turned to walk away down the hill, raising my hand and re-initiating Kronos's need to crawl through filth and failure.

His raspy laughter made me pause and turn. "What's on your mind?"

"We didn't decide the timeline for her creation. There wasn't a delay. She happened right when she needed to."

I crouched down, deadly intent in my glare. "Who decided then?"

His laughter redoubled. "A force far beyond you."

A small chill stole through me. He couldn't mean— "Nobody's heard a peep from them since before the wars began. They abandoned us all."

Kronos continued to laugh. I raised my hand and clenched my fist and his body contorted painfully but still he laughed. No matter how much I tried to elicit a scream of agony all I got was gleeful howling.

I snarled and gave up, walking briskly away, his amusement ringing through the whole chamber. As I reached the bottom of the hill he roared, "You can't beat Fate!"

All the Titans joined in the laughter, and as I reached the gates to leave Tartarus, I was surrounded by the ringing chorus.

You can't beat Fate.

CHAPTER SEVENTEEN

Gareth

This was it, my chance to get through to her. There was little hostility in the set of her shoulders. I'd noticed that she always squared them up when she was ready for a fight.

But now she sat next to me, almost completely at ease. Stress and anxiety still tore at her, but that was a given with the horrors she'd just witnessed. Even though I'd seen worse—much worse—in my long life, seeing my family destroyed brought to life old wounds that I'd thought I'd hardened myself against a long time ago.

"Well, why don't we start with who you really are and how you found yourself in their service?" she asked.

I looked down as I cast back in my memory. "You'll have to forgive me if my storytelling skills are rough. It's been a long time since I've had to recall any of this."

Latching on to a fond moment, I started with that. "When I was a young man, I conscripted into a shifter legion comprised of Celtic tribes that had settled in the Alps. We'd been tasked with holding off an invading army of Etruscans."

"Rome before it was Rome?" she asked.

I smiled. "Yes. You know your history."

Excitement lit up her face and my smile grew to match it. "I love ancient history. I always tell myself that I'll go back and visit all these places after—" Her face fell, guilt written all over it.

"Meg, you don't need to be ashamed. You thought you were doing the right thing."

"I only feel guilty because of my plans toward you. I'm still not convinced about the Titans," she said, rotating her shoulders to work out a kink.

"Let's see if I can change that," I replied easily. "Most of us had no idea what we were doing. A man in my battalion, Remi, was like a brother to me."

"Is he one of the Six?" Meg asked.

I tsked. "No jumping ahead."

She snorted softly and nodded.

"Remi and I soon worked our way up the ranks and the time came when we were offered positions as commanders of our own legions. War with the Etruscans was mostly just the occasional skirmish at this point. They were too busy with Rome and times of peace stretched out before us for months and then years. Remi and I spent most of our time doing what young men do when they don't have more pressing matters to attend to, even men of our rank."

"Peace must've been rare. I don't blame you."

"It was." I reached over and grabbed some pine cones, tossing them aimlessly into the fire and listening to them pop.

"Eventually the time came when we'd be called to action. The enemy was not what any of us would've expected."

My face darkened. I could smell the fires all over again, hear the screams. "My city was collateral damage. Caught in the middle as the gods brought their wars to the mortal plane. We were helpless to stop them."

Meg was watching me closely, her face revealing nothing, but her pulse had quickened.

"Remi and I did our best to organize defenses, but our two battalions were the only ones that survived those initial days. We were vastly outnumbered and safe places were running out. We had to make hard decisions about who we could save and who we had to leave behind."

"Oh," Meg whispered. She worried her lip again and plucked at that odd amulet around her neck.

"It was going into the third week of the siege—"

"An actual siege? Against Ætherim?"

Good, she was still able to be objective. "No. I call it that not because they were attacking us directly, but because we had no way to get out. They were fighting around us and over us and turning the city to rubble and the land to waste without even noticing we were there. We were sheltering as best we could, as far underground as we could get. Our last reserves were running out and the tunnel we used to get to our water source had just collapsed. We all thought we were going to die."

"But the Titans came?" she asked. Her voice was a whisper, I almost couldn't hear it over the crackling fire. I wondered if she realized how far toward me she was leaning.

I nodded. "Yes." I tore my eyes away from her lips and the dusting of freckles across her cheeks that were glowing in the firelight.

"There was a sudden, deafening silence. The world had stopped shaking, the cries of the Ætherim weren't echoing through every waking moment. When we stepped out into the daylight again, our city was mostly rubble, and a great dome was circling it. Outside it we could see a battle continuing. But along with the giant fiery forms of the gods, there were new arrivals. Giants, larger than the Ætherim."

My eyes clouded with tears as I remembered my first sight of the Titans. "Even more terrible to witness. They were beings of indescribable power. The Ætherim had stopped fighting among themselves and were now standing united against these entities. And the survivors, we all watched it play out, convinced that at any moment the entire battle would turn on us. Or that perhaps the dome sheltering us was only in place so they could keep us alive for food. We weren't ignorant of the habits of their forebears.

"I'd heard legends retold by my family about the giant cities thousands of years before our great civilization, that had been centers of worship and sacrifice to the Ancients and the Great Elementals before those creatures were cast out and the Elementals were sealed within the earth, their power dissolved into the land where it belonged.

"But none of that happened. The Titans were the victors. When the dome was removed, they greeted us. It was a spectacle, to be sure. Giant beings shrinking down to our size as they stepped across a field still wet with blood."

"They could make themselves that small?" asked Meg.

I nodded, chuckling. "I would later come to learn that they had to siphon off huge amounts of their power to another plane to do it. Otherwise they would have just burst out of their skins."

"So what did they say?"

Her face was so close now, I could see the gem-colored facets sparkling in her eyes. She was breathtaking. "They introduced themselves, told us not to be afraid. The threat was over. They offered to help us rebuild."

"In exchange for what?" Meg's voice held no hint of derision or disbelief, it was a simple question.

"Nothing," I said.

Meg blinked. "Nothing at all?"

I shook my head. "Not a thing. They helped us bury our dead, find food, water. When we decided we couldn't stay, they helped us on our travels to locate new homes. They only wanted to help undo the damage the gods had done."

"Why?"

"They'd been watching the human realm for millennia, both the Strangers and the mortals within it. They were constantly awed with the accomplishments we made in our communities. Back then, Strangers and humans lived side by side with little conflict, mostly in the open. And the cities we built because of it, the inventions, the artistic undertakings... they wanted to see that continue.

"And they knew without protection from the wars the Ætherim were waging amongst themselves in their power struggles that bled over into our realm far too often, humanity and lesser Strangers wouldn't stand a chance of survival. The gods would have been fine remaking the world from scratch, but the Titans couldn't let that happen. Especially not if the Ætherim had uncontested power."

"What was happening in the Strangefells during all this?" Meg asked.

"I can't say from experience, I only set foot there a few times. But it's my understanding that the Strangefells was little more than a wasteland. It had been neglected in the beginning by the earliest inhabitants because their preferred food source was in the human realm."

Meg suppressed a shudder of disgust.

"Then it became a battleground, one giant arena for the elder beings to settle their differences or pit lesser Strangers against each other for sport. By the time I was born, it had started to display signs of settlement, villages starting to crop up here and there. Still worlds away from anything the mortal realm possessed. But once humans began to reject us—" Bitterness coated my words.

"Things in the Strangefells developed at an exponential rate?" Meg finished.

"Yes."

"So what did you do for the Titans?" she asked.

I considered my answer. It wasn't so defined that there could be a simple explanation. "At first, Remi and I made sure the other survivors got settled. Most of our battalions had died, leaving us with only a few troops and no city to fight for anyway. We spent a couple of years in the trades. Remi decided to travel with a merchant crew, to provide protection on the roads. I chose to join the city guard. It's all we've ever really been good for."

Involuntarily, my eyes drifted back in the direction of the caravan. "Until now."

I jumped when Meg's fingers brushed my own and she moved closer still. She sat shoulder to shoulder with me and twined her arm in mine, rejoining our hands. A thrill moved through me.

Her breath whispered against my skin as she rested her head on my bicep. "It's not your fault."

"Then whose is it?" I asked harshly. "It was my job to protect them."

"We were all outnumbered. The odds were overwhelmingly against us."

"That doesn't change the fact that I failed them!" I roared, and Meg scrambled back. Regret replaced the anger, and I reached for her but she scurried farther still, staring at my outstretched hand and clutching at her forearm. My claws had elongated in my loss of control. I'd hurt her.

"I'm so sorry, Meg," I said, willing my claws to change back to normal fingers. As they receded, I took tentative steps toward her, hoping I hadn't ruined the delicate companionship we'd managed to form. The fear in her eyes killed me.

"Can I take a look?" I asked, holding out a clawless hand.

Her gaze flicked from my face to my hand several times before she nodded jerkily and held out her own hand. I crouched next to her and pushed her sleeve away but the cuts were already knitting together. I hummed gratefully. "You heal even faster than I do."

Meg pulled away and swiped a hand across her arm as the last of the cuts healed, smearing the blood and adding it to the rest of the bloodstains on her dress. She slid her sleeve back down and hugged her arms to herself.

I gave her some space and retreated to the fire, continuing my story.

"After a couple of years passed, I got tired of the routine. My mind kept wandering to the Titans. Thinking that I could serve a better purpose if I joined them."

She snorted again, but it was more derisive this time. "Why would you think they'd need help from a shifter? They're Titans."

I shook my head. "I honestly wasn't sure. Something was calling to me, so I decided to try to find them, offer my service and see what happened."

"What if it was all a ploy? And you were playing into their hand?"

I fired back this time. "Why would they need to play games with a lowly shifter?"

"I never said lowly," Meg grumbled, inching closer to the fire.

"I sent word to Remi of my plans. I knew he was as restless as I was, so there was a good chance that he'd join me on the journey. He did."

The fire spat as it found a crevice of moisture in one the logs I'd added. A chill stole over me that had nothing to do with the cool night air.

Meg was beside me again. "And what did you find?"

I hesitated. "Greatness."

CHAPTER EIGHTEEN

Meg

Gareth's stories had given me a lot to think about. We had settled next to the fire to make an attempt at sleep, but my mind wouldn't slow down.

I barely gave any thought to the incident with his loss of control. There was no question that it was an accident; the grief on his face when he'd realized what happened convinced me of that.

But listening to his tales was difficult. It put everything I thought I knew on its head. It couldn't be that way, how would the lore have been so wrong?

Because the victors write the history.

Bel had never been one to choose humility when it came to retelling tales of how he'd beaten the Titans. But the idea that they were truly innocent, only wanting to help without any ulterior motive stuck in my craw. That didn't make sense, just on the simple level that beings that powerful never do anything for free. The older they get, the more they need entertainment, and they have terrible ways of going about it.

But what did that say for Bel? I'd already begun to see parts of him that didn't mesh with the man I thought I knew. There was a darkness in him, sure, but a cruel streak had made itself plain and he couldn't say it was just because of the stress.

A week ago I'd have said I loved him, but now... I didn't know. If I could compare it even a little to what I felt when I was around Arthur and Gareth—not including the lust, but everything else—I wasn't sure what I felt for Bel could ever have been considered love. I was comfortable. He made me feel safe. But that was quickly going out the window, and I had to wonder how much of his behavior was simply to manipulate me. Neither him nor the Titans were innocent of that.

What game was he playing? And what would he do if I refused to keep playing it?

The deepest into sleep I got was a light doze, and when I heard movement, I came out of it quickly.

"Is it time to move on?" I asked, rubbing my eyes and looking around, expecting to find Gareth.

It was still the middle of the night. More sounds, like several pairs of approaching footsteps. Shit.

The first of the human warriors broke into the clearing, a grin on his face. His voice was a low growl that promised pain and death. "Found you."

Two more appeared to my left, more to my right and I could hear more behind me. Where was Gareth?

"What do you want? Who are you?"

"Don't even try to fool us, witch! You're not human," spat another man, brandishing his single-bladed axe. "You'll die like the rest of those evil—"

I never would find out the end of that sentence, not that I was brokenhearted about it. Clawed hands reached out of the darkness and yanked the man back. He screamed briefly before the sound cut off.

The other men were still staring in shock at the place where their buddy had been when the man's axe came flying out of the darkness and landed squarely in the chest of one of the mortals behind me. He keeled over and I sprang toward him, wrenching the axe free.

Gareth growled as he launched himself into the clearing, swiping madly with his claws, his form transfigured once again into the half man, half wolf. He tore out one man's throat, and I jumped into the battle, swinging at the nearest warrior, and cleaving his head down the middle.

I caught another across the throat as he dodged backward, not quick enough to avoid me, and used the momentum to swing the axe around over my head and throw it forward into the chest of another right before Gareth could take him out.

"Is that all?" I asked, somewhat disappointed as I looked around at the fallen bodies. Gareth had killed most of them but at least I got the last warrior standing.

In the second it took for me to look away and back again, Gareth had returned to his human form. He rushed over to me and gripped my shoulders. "Are you alright?"

I blinked at him. "Did you not notice the guy that I brained lying over there?"

He grinned and then laughed in relief. "Of course, what was I thinking?"

We set to work moving the bodies and traveled a short distance to a stream to wash the blood off as best we could.

Our clothes were ruined, but there was no way around it at the moment.

"Did you think I'd abandoned you?" Gareth asked once we'd settled back by the fire. He sounded wary.

"No," I said, scooting closer to him. Gareth's eyes widened in surprise. "I thought maybe they'd decided to double down on being cowards and waited to attack until you stepped away."

Gareth eased his arm around me, and I leaned into him. "I heard them coming and snuck out of camp so I could double back behind them. I didn't plan on you joining in, but I'm glad you did. You looked like a warrior queen, wielding that axe. We'll have to get you some tattoos."

I reached over and stroked along the lines of his own tattoos, feeling him shudder as I did so. "I'd like that."

His eyes focused on me so intently, my palms started to sweat. Every fiber of my being wanted to wrap my arm around his neck and kiss him just to hear the growl he'd make low in his throat.

My face flushed, and I was burning up. Gareth moved closer, only an inch of space separating us. My breath hitched and Gareth lifted his other hand to cradle my face. I turned my head slightly and licked the tip of his thumb, taking it into my mouth and sucking on it, tongue swirling. Showing him I wasn't afraid of the claws that hid beneath.

That growl I longed to hear rumbled up from Gareth's chest. I released his thumb, unable to speak, my thoughts consumed by the heat of his presence and wanting to feel the weight of him as he settled over me.

He captured my mouth with his. When his tongue parted my lips and swept through my mouth, tasting me, I leaned into it. His arms wrapped around me, and he pulled me into his lap as I settled one knee on either side of his thighs. I squeezed my knees around his waist and pushed my breasts into his searching hands, wrapping my arms around his neck.

The bulge in his tartan pressed against my thighs and I switched my hips, grinding against him. Gareth bit my lower lip with a light nip that was completely contrary to the fierce growl that rose from his chest and the lust in his eyes.

An owl called in the distance and my head snapped toward it, but Gareth's firm hand turned my face back to his. He bucked his hips, pushing right at my center and tearing a gasp from my throat. He was driving me wild, and we still had all our clothes on.

I kissed him, already thinking of the possibilities. Looking forward to the relief of finally being satisfied.

Gareth's fingers dove between us. He grazed my clit, and I bit his lip at the teasing. He settled into a rhythm, and I was quickly reaching a peak when one finger, then two slid into my entrance. I groaned and jerked my hips, riding his hand as he stretched me open with a third. He pumped his fingers as I rode, his thumb returning to my nub in slow circles until I came with a shout.

Some more commotion and a breeze swirled through the clearing. A strange sensation like an icy hand reached into my chest as I came down slowly. Gareth moved his fingers away, and I started to shift his kilt aside.

I felt a tug and the time stream opened around me, but instead of being a relief it only elicited a shock of fear. I wasn't controlling it.

"Fuck," I cursed.

"Aye, that's what I'm trying to do." Gareth's hands tightened on my hips as he held me to him, a desperation in his eyes.

"No," I panted, patting his face so he'd snap out of it. "Something's wrong."

He immediately snapped back to attention, and I slid off his lap. He leaped to his feet, ready to defend me against whatever might be out there. But this attacker couldn't be seen.

"Someone's trying to pull me through time."

"What? How?" he asked.

I shook my head as the amulet around my neck started to glow. I grabbed for it, struggling to yank it off my neck, but it wouldn't break.

"Meg, what's—"

And then a hard tug in the middle of my chest had me catapulting through time, landing heavily at Bel's feet.

CHAPTER NINETEEN

Meg

The smile that greeted me was not one of welcoming. It was cruel, predatory. It promised pain. I threw myself backward and scuttled away, but Bel followed and grabbed the front of my bloodied dress, hauling me to my feet.

"Looks like you've had quite an adventure." Bel grasped the amulet and tore it from my neck. His nostrils flared as he scented me, and his pupils dilated. He pushed me away from him and I stumbled, landing hard on my ass. "Did you bond?" he snarled.

I shook my head frantically. "No."

"Then why do I smell sex and a wolf shifter on you?" he spat, looming over me, his rage taking up the entire space around us and making his presence suffocating.

"We-we didn't get that far." My whole body trembled in fear. I'd seen his anger, but not like this.

Movement in the background caught my eye, and I saw Risha and Ursal hovering, waiting for orders. They looked just as terrified as I was, and both were sporting injuries that were still healing.

"How did you bring me back?" I asked.

Bel sneered and leaned down, hinging at the waist until he was peering into my face, his breath hot and sour. "You don't get to ask questions." His fingers clawed at me through the fabric as he dragged me to my feet again. "You've disobeyed me for the last time." His voice was a whisper. "You've never known pain like what's waiting for you now."

My toes scuffed along the floor as he carried me across the room to the door that led to the subbasement. The heavy bolt slid back, and we descended.

"Bel, please, let me explain!" I begged. "It's not what you think! I was going to send him back, I just—"

The breath whooshed from my lungs as he slammed me into the wall, my head cracking on the cold concrete. Stars burst through my vision and gorge surged up my throat.

"Not... another... word."

At the bottom of the stairs, we took a left and passed into a narrow hallway where he unlocked a smaller door and slid back three extra bolts. This one was made of solid iron. It didn't affect me like it would have done with fae or another closely related Stranger, but I could feel its heavy presence, nonetheless.

The room was dark with only faint light trickling from a small shaft cut high in the ceiling and slanting away toward the surface that was circulating fresh air throughout the chamber, keeping the scent of blood, fear, and bodily waste to a minimum.

Overhead lights flared to life, and I suddenly wished that I'd remained in the dark. The room was cluttered with all manner of devices that gleamed cruelly under the harsh LEDs. Some of the items that lined shelves or stood against walls I only recognized from books on medieval torture methods. And there were plenty of things I didn't recognize that scared me even more.

In the middle of the room was a cage only large enough to sit up or lay flat in with shackles inside it. We bypassed every-thing else, and Bel wrenched open the door of the cage and threw me in, reaching in to bind the shackles around my ankles. He slammed the cage shut and cut off the lights before he left the room, the iron door closing behind him with an awful finality.

My breath was coming in short gasps and my body was still shaking with the adrenaline and fear. I hugged myself into a ball and lay on the metal grate with the cold concrete seeping through my dress and making the shivering worse.

There must have been iron bands running all through the walls, ceiling, and floor because I couldn't tap into the bit of magick I did possess, let alone the stream of time. I was cut off, altogether at Bel's mercy. How could I have been so stupid? I wanted to believe him. He'd made me feel less alone, like he understood what it meant to be used, like we were doing something that the whole world would benefit from, even if they couldn't know.

He'd taken a lonely, confused girl away from a miserable life and given her a chance to prove herself. And I fell for it, hook, line, and sinker. I hadn't wanted to see the many red flags that would have outed him as a liar and a manipulator the same way I'd ignored the blatant lies about the "gilded cage" the living links were being sent to.

Now here I was, in an actual cage. Waiting to find out whatever fate he might have in store for me. The spell he'd had over me was broken, and I'd woken up to a nightmare.

"What else do you know! Where are they!" Bel had to yell over the hum of the extricator. It had been his favorite device to use so far. He'd grab me out of my cage at least three times a day and strap me to a table flat on my back. Several stone needles were inserted into my body at pulse points, but that pain barely even registered, they were so sharp. It was what came after.

"Nothing!" I sobbed. Another round of magick coursed through my body, a combination of being dipped in liquid fire, electrocuted, and having the flesh torn from your body, with acid tossed on the open wounds. It was so complete a pain that every molecule of my being felt like it was being shredded and picked apart.

"I've told you everything!"

"Liar!"

"No! No, I'm not! I've told you—" I panted. "—everything." The pain subsided and my treacherous body went to work healing itself, but the process was slower every passing day. My body was clammy and while I wasn't sure what a fever felt like, I had a suspicion that I had one. The torture was taking its toll.

Bel, lip curled in disgust, threw me back in my cage and locked me in. I dozed, my dreams becoming so strange I couldn't tell waking from sleeping anymore.

Later that evening—at least, I think it was evening, the light never wavered much—Ursal came to bring me some food. It was more of a gesture than anything, as I didn't need food to survive.

Ursal unlocked the door and my shackles before touching my shoulder to shake me awake. If Bel knew he and Risha did that, he would've been furious, but it was the one kindness they could risk.

Groggy eyes, full of sleep and crusted over, fought to stay open as I grasped Ursal's wrist, disregarding the plate of food he'd set down. I looked into his eyes, pleading.

"Just kill me. Please."

His face fell, and a grieved smile came to his face. "You can't give in to those thoughts, Meg. Give him what he wants, and this will be over."

"There is nothing else." I hated how desperate the words sounded. "I've told him about Gareth, but I can't access time anymore. Even if I knew where any of the others were, I couldn't get them, so what does he hope to gain?"

Risha told me they'd used the amulet to track me, and Bel had spent an enormous amount of power to bring me back. But the effort had left him weak. He wouldn't risk doing that again, let alone five more times.

Ursal felt my face and his brow creased in concern. "You're ill."

"My body can't take much more of this."

He retrieved a rag and rinsed it in some cold water, mopping my face. The sensation was heavenly, and I leaned into him, closing my eyes.

"Risha might have found a way."

Dread started its slow creep into my gut, and I forced my eyes open again. "She has? How?"

Ursal shook his head, looking hopeful. "She's still working it out, but she has evidence that it's possible. Then Bel can track the others down and you'll be free."

He sounded so convinced. He still didn't see what was happening here. "No, I won't. Once he has the others, he won't need me. I'm the last link. There's only one way this is going to end."

His face shut down, and I recognized my own stubbornness and methods of mental gymnastics that I used to get around facing the truth.

"No. You'll see. Once Risha figures it out. You'll see." He couldn't hide the shaking in his hands as he refastened the shackles and took the untouched plate of food away, shutting the door. Before retreating from the room, he paused and looked back at me, pressed against the side of the cage, digging my fingers into my palms to keep focus on him through the fever haze clouding my mind.

"Bel does love you. This is only what's necessary."

And he was gone.

I floated in some kind of half-aware state, I have no idea for how long, with Bel coming by for his usual sessions with the extricator. Now I couldn't even answer him if I wanted to.

The only thing that registered a little was when Risha came down as Bel was throwing me back in my cage to give him news that she'd discovered something. Bel gave a triumphant shout and ran out of the room, slamming the door behind him, and I was left in darkness for what felt like much longer than usual. Only faintly did the thought cross my mind that I hadn't heard the locks slide into place.

She must've figured it out. That meant time was running out for all of us. Bel would either leave me here to die in this cage or more likely he'd wait until he had all the Desma—no, my mates—captured so he could kill them in front of me before putting me out of my misery.

I'd betrayed Gareth. Bel would get him first.

No, wait.

There was another man I'd betrayed before him.

Guilt and heartache overrode the sickness. Arthur. In all the whirlwind that had happened since Gareth had revealed the answers to so many of my questions, I hadn't had a chance to think about Arthur. The man I'd sent to his death. The man who would have been my mate.

I'd felt that connection to Arthur just the same, and his behavior right before I sent him back made much more sense now.

I'd killed him. I'd been so blinded by Bel and the lies I wanted to believe that I'd killed my own mate. How could I face any of the others ever again, even if I did get out of here? What kind of monster does that to someone they're meant to love? Even in that brief moment I knew him, I had started to love him.

The fever found me in my grief and self-hatred and pulled me into a restless sleep.

I drifted.

Everything was gray.

The clouds began to disperse, and I felt a new energy in me, like I'd been revitalized.

And I was back in my dungeon. But I was looking at my body.

Had I died?

I looked closer and saw my chest rising and falling, my whole body covered in a sheen of sweat. I reached for my body and my hand began to pass through the solid bars of the enclosure, but got stuck halfway. I pulled my hand back with a sucking sensation and was soon free. I reached toward my prison again and my hand ran into the bars as if they were solid.

My eyes shot to the keys hanging on the wall and moved for them, trying to figure out how to pilot this spectral form. After some work, I figured it out and was able to lift the keys from the wall, but my hand lost form and the keys fell to the floor with a clatter. I froze, listening hard for any sign that someone outside had heard. When there was no movement, I focused all my will on making my hand solid again and this time I kept hold of the keys.

The cage door swung open on well-oiled and well-used hinges and the shackles fell away. I floated back to the main door and tried to push through it, but the iron prevented me from passing through and scrambled my spectral body so badly I woke up back in my real body.

The heaviness settled over me again, the sickness still rampaging freely. That iron door was the only thing between me and freedom, but the locks were on the outside.

Then I remembered that I hadn't heard those locks when Bel rushed out. Could it really be unlocked? I took a deep breath and crawled toward the exit, every inch feeling like a mile.

My hand brushed against the handle but I couldn't quite reach. I struggled to support my weight with one arm as I lifted myself up higher, my arm trembling underneath me and threatening to give out.

But at last my fingers wrapped around the handle and I pulled. The door popped open a fraction, and I collapsed back with a sigh, a weak laugh escaping lungs still raw from screaming.

I regathered my strength and clawed at the door from my position, lying flat on the floor. It opened farther, the only sound being the latch as it sprang free from the doorframe.

Once I could fit through, I crawled, dragging my body across the smooth concrete until I was out of that iron cage. I struggled to catch my breath and stared at the ceiling, willing any sign of the time stream to come to me.

And without hesitation, it did.

Tears welled in my eyes, and I slapped a hand to my mouth to stifle the sobs that tore from my throat. Time flowed around me, wrapping me in its embrace, welcoming me back.

Gareth.

The flow of time swept around me and carried me away.

Chapter Twenty

Gareth

She'd disappeared right in front of me, and I couldn't do anything to stop it. I'd felt every trace of her disappear from my awareness, like she'd never been.

I sat by the fire, numb with loss and confusion. How could that have happened? Very few beings can affect time, and even fewer are able to move people through it. What had Bel gotten his hands on now?

And what was I supposed to do? I couldn't follow, couldn't protect her. I was worthless. Belsioch would know of her treachery against him the minute he saw her and there was no telling what he would do. If he didn't need her for time travel, he'd kill her and come after us next.

Hopelessness crashed over me then. All of it was for nothing. He'd found a way to best us after all.

So I focused on the only thing I could; the world I was living in. This camp was compromised, it was time to move on. That was an immediate, actionable plan, and it was as far as my mind could be bothered to think ahead.

I packed up what little I had and started off. The journey to another camp I'd used as a lone wolf was only two days' travel if I didn't stop for more than an hour at a time and moved in my wolf form. I'd strapped my belongings to my back and shifted, leaving a long strap end that I could tighten with my teeth. And so I set off.

The rains were harsh and a major storm rolled through, but I ran on. I didn't care; let a landslide smother me or lightning strike me. There was nothing left for me anymore.

When I reached my camp, soaked through to the bone, I changed back and went about building a fire. I'd welcome death when it came for me, but I wouldn't rush into its arms.

Taking a bite of bear jerky, I couldn't help but smile, recalling Meg's reaction when I'd teased her about it being human. I drank enough mead to lure me into a heavy sleep and let the dreams drag me down.

A soft cry of pain broke through my dreams of holding Meg in my arms, bonding with her, fighting alongside her. I blinked into the darkness, the smoldering embers of the fire providing just enough light to cast eerie shadows. My heart leaped when I realized I wasn't alone and who the new arrival was.

Another soft sound rustled in the brush nearby and I bounded to my feet, rushing to her. I tore a path through gorse and bramble and found her lying face down, her body limp and pale.

"Meg!" The name came out with a strangled cry as I bent and lifted her into my arms, cradling her to my chest. She felt so light, and so hot. Her face had become gaunt, and her veins stood out starkly against her skin. I could hear a faint pulse and feel a soft breath against my shoulder, but she made no more sound.

I rushed her back to the fire and stoked the flames, tossing on fuel and bringing them up to roaring. Checking her over for injuries, I found none, bodily anyway. But she was burning with fever. There was a small pool and waterfall nearby that flowed into a long tributary that fed one of the trade canals.

The full moon overhead provided enough light to pick my way over the rocks onto the sandy shore. I stripped away her ruined clothing and my own before walking us into the water until she was submerged up to her neck. A groan escaped her when the cold water hit, but I kept walking around, moving the water around her body and helping her acclimate.

Her body began to shiver, but I persisted. I was no healer, but I knew that it was her sickness fighting back, struggling to claim her. I crushed her to me and pinched her nose closed with my fingers before dunking her under. Her hair flowed around her in the water, catching the moonlight and turning pure silver, dazzling light pouring from it with the water in runnels when I lifted her up. I poured my own power into her, urging her body to regenerate.

After several more rounds of dunking her under, she finally opened her eyes.

Relief flooded me as I smiled down at her, clearing hair from her face. "There you are."

Meg grinned at me weakly. "I found you."

It sounded painful for her to speak. I carried her out of the water and wrapped her in a blanket I'd brought, sitting on the sandy shore and cradling her in my arms like I'd never let her go.

Her shivering had ceased, and her body felt cool. She'd fallen asleep, her breathing even and smooth instead of pained and ragged. I didn't realize how long we'd been sitting there until the sun started to come up.

Meg finally roused from sleep when the first rays of sunlight broke into the cove. Her lips split into a smile. "Gareth."

I helped her sit up, and she looked around, her eyes settling on her reflection in the water. The gauntness in her face had almost filled back in, but the circles under her eyes were dark and heavy and the look in her eyes told of horrible things.

"What happened?" I asked, once her attention moved away from her self-evaluation. Part of me was afraid to hear what else I hadn't been able to protect her from.

Her breath hitched. "Bel—" She suddenly remembered something and began to panic. "He knows how to travel through time, they've figured it out. They'll find us!" Her face became stricken. "I told him where you were. I never thought he'd be able to get to you." Tears started to fall down her cheeks. "I just wanted the pain to stop."

Rage prickled up from the base of my spine until it was a swirling torrent in my chest. "What did he do to you?" I asked.

Her voice was only a whisper. "The extricator. It was his favorite tool."

A snarl so ferocious tore from my throat that Meg bit back a cry of surprise and almost toppled out of my arms.

She nodded. "So you're familiar."

"Aye." When I saw the fear and pain written over every inch of her body, I softened. I didn't need to make this worse by focusing on my anger. I needed her to know she was safe.

"We have to find the others. Have you regained enough strength to transport us both?"

"No. I can probably get us halfway."

"You should rest. We'll only go when you're strong enough."

"But what if they find us? You can't fight them all."

"It's a chance we'll have to take. But this cove is decently well protected and there are underground caverns where we can lose them if it comes to it. What do you think is the likelihood he'd be able to figure it out quickly, even with help?"

Meg considered. "Things Risha develops are often easiest for her to use or operate. Other people need a lot more time to learn it. And she was rushing through it." She shrugged. "And some part of me hopes that she'll slow him down on purpose. I don't think she bought into Bel's lies the same way her brother did."

I nodded. "Then we'll focus on getting you back to full health."

Meg nodded and chewed her lip. She was bracing herself for something and moved to free herself from the blanket. I helped her, hesitant. This seemed serious, and compared to what she'd already told me, I wasn't sure what to expect.

She knelt in front of me and stared at her hands. "There's something else you should know. You might rethink your choice to have saved me."

I placed my hand under her chin and lifted her face to meet mine. "Nothing you say could make me regret that."

She still couldn't look me in the eye. "I've already found Arthur. Before I came to find you."

My body froze and the stillness made Meg lean away. She spoke fast. "I was desperate to prove myself, so I finally took the leap and searched for a Desma with my own signature. I wanted a prize to give to Bel to make him see that my heart was still with the mission. With him," she hissed, clenching her fists.

Fresh tears fell. "I found him and I felt a similar connection as I do to you. But—I didn't let myself believe it. I thought he was fooling me. I ignored all the signs that said he was telling the truth."

Meg bent over double as a sob racked her body. "He begged me not to send him away. He told me Bel was the enemy, and I didn't listen."

Her words were almost inaudible past guilt-driven wails.

"I looked him in the eye, and I sent him to his death!" she cried, her voice breaking. Her eyes lifted finally to meet mine, and they were full of raw grief and so, so much guilt.

"And you're certain he's dead," I asked, tone flat.

Meg shuddered and took a breath. "Bel didn't say it explicitly, but it was strongly implied. And I believe I saw his spirit."

She lurched forward and grabbed my hands. "I'm so sorry, Gareth." She shook her head and hiccoughed. "I don't expect you to forgive me, but please know how sorry I am."

I pulled my hands away. The crestfallen look on Meg's face wrenched my heart.

"Don't misunderstand, Meg." I hurried to wrap my arms around her and pull her back in, tucking her head under my chin. "I'm heartbroken at what you did." She shrank in my grasp. "But I'm not angry at you. I'm furious at the man who forced you to do it."

"But he didn't. I chose every step of the way."

I shook my head even though she couldn't see it. "You didn't choose. He manipulated you. All the worst of them get into your head and make you think you're living a life of free will, so you're complicit in your own abuse. To blame it on you."

Tears fell freely down my face. "It is not... your... fault. This was Belsioch, all of it."

"But wouldn't that apply to everything, then? Nothing we do is free from the influence of other people." She was still determined to take the blame.

"How many other people do you have in your life?" I asked her.

She paused. "Just Bel and the twin nephilim that work with us."

"Was that your choice, or his?"

A longer pause. "I don't really have time for a social life. We did go out places."

"But he was always with you?"

Her fingers clenched in her lap. "Yes."

"He was your whole world, by design. Your only influence. Your only confidant."

The words hurt me to say. Even thinking about what she must've been through before Belsioch showed his true face was sickening and I wanted to get my claws into him so badly, I could taste his blood.

"It was still me that betrayed Arthur. Betrayed all of you, in a way."

"And we'll all have to live with that, but it still wasn't your fault." I leaned in and kissed her briefly. "For what it's worth, I forgive you, even though you don't need it. And I'm sure Arthur knew that you weren't acting on your own." My voice cracked. "He was always perceptive like that."

Meg freed her arms from me and threw them around my neck, hugging me tightly.

It was difficult for me to process how she made me feel. Even though I knew that this was a true-mate bond, I wasn't ready for the overwhelming emotions. The desire to protect and defend her with my life was a given. But the tenderness toward her, the need for her to feel safe and happy in my arms... We'd just met but there was so much more to it than lust.

While some things would take getting used to, one thing was certain. I wasn't letting anyone hurt her again. I'd give my last breath to keep her away from Belsioch.

CHAPTER TWENTY-ONE

Gareth

"So tell me more about this true-mate bond. What's going to happen when we finally—you know." She was leaning against me, arm draped along the top of my leg with her hand resting on my knee.

"Not getting shy on me now, are you?" I asked her, teasing. The last couple of days she'd recovered most of her strength and the time was almost right to travel. To find another of my long-lost brothers-in-arms. But there was one thing we needed to accomplish first.

We were sitting by the water pool again. It had become some kind of revered place for us since, in a way, it was where we got each other back.

"I didn't want to scandalize your delicate sensibilities," she said with a laugh. As if to prove her point, her hand slid down my thigh, torturously close to my cock.

I growled at her sly smile, taking a shaky breath and trying my best to focus.

"There was no small amount of chance that went into your creation. The Titans themselves could only put their magick into action and see what happened. It was ultimately in the hands of the Fates. You could have taken any form, human, inhuman, amorphous blob of goo," I said, smiling. "And we would have protected you no matter what." I touched her cheek.

"But the Fates were smiling on us all when they intervened with you. Not only did they create a stunning beauty, but they turned that bond between us into something more than just a duty to protect. That fire we feel—"

I broke off, staring into her eyes.

"What, Gareth?" she breathed.

"There's no doubt in my mind. I know it the same way that I knew your name. I sensed it when we first met across time. The Fates gave you the charge of being the key to the Titans' freedom, but they also gifted us in the process. That bond... is a true-mate bond."

"How—" But she couldn't finish the question. What I'd said had struck a chord with her.

"As far as my understanding goes—and mind you, this is all what I've learned from others that were in very different situations—that connection we have now will grow strong enough that we'll perceive each other's emotions, discern where the other is anywhere in this world if we focus in. And we'll be able to draw on each other's power."

"So you'll be able to tap into time?" Meg's brow was knit.

I shook my head. "No. It's more like what I did when I was trying to revive you. When I was touching you, I could transfer power to you, to help you heal. Once we're bonded, we'll sense the other's need and can send magick through that connection, no matter how far away we are from each other."

"Oh."

I inched away so I could see her face. "Are you having second thoughts?"

Her eyes widened and she shook her head. "No, not at all." A smile crept in, and she snuggled closer. "I'm just trying to wrap my brain around it. I've already never felt this close to anyone, even when that dickface had me fooled."

"Dickface," I mused. "Not familiar with the term, but it has a ring to it that fits that monster perfectly."

Her nails scratched at my knee absentmindedly. "Everything in me is telling me I belong. Like I have a true place, with people that are more of a home than any physical house. I'm looking forward to it. But if I'm being honest, I'm not sure I entirely trust it."

My heart swelled, not put off by her reservations. She'd been burned so many times, I couldn't blame her. "Then I'll have to prove to you every day that you can. That no matter what happens, our family will be unbreakable. Unstoppable."

Meg sighed and looked back at the water. "Family." She fidgeted and I heard a grin in her voice. "One thing I am curious about, though," she continued.

I hummed in response.

"I've never been a very territorial lover. But aren't the lot of you going to be alpha personalities?"

I inclined my head. "Yes. But unless they've changed immensely since I last knew them, it won't be a problem. The way I think about it is, you're my mate—"

Meg drew in a quick breath.

"Something wrong?" I asked.

"Not at all," she purred. "I just loved how that sounded."

I chuckled and kissed the patch of skin behind her ear. "Good. Because as my mate, I know that what we share is untouchable. There's no need for jealousy. They are all good, honorable men, and we're all charged with your wellbeing. I'm happy to participate in group activities, and get plenty of time with you on my own."

Meg shuddered and raised her hand to skim her nails over my beard. The warrior rings woven through the strands jingled and fire kindled under my skin. "I can be pretty insatiable," she breathed, running her lips down the side of my jaw. "You'll all have a lot to keep up with."

"We'll make sure you're plenty satisfied, don't you worry."

She pulled away from me and repositioned herself, straddling my lap. She wrapped her arms around my neck. "Is there anything special we need to do to initiate it?"

I shook my head. "Not a thing. But are you sure you're ready? I don't want to compromise your healing."

"Never been more sure of anything." Her lips crashed against mine and she melted into me, lowering herself to grind her hips.

My lips moved to her neck, and she bared it for me again. I growled in approval and my teeth grazed the thin skin. She shuddered and bucked against me, tilting her head all the way to the side to expose her throat.

My tongue traced her clavicle, and I placed kisses along her chin before dipping my head back down to lick and nip at the hollow of her throat. I nuzzled my nose behind her ear and she moaned, straining against my cock. I moved my mouth to that spot and her breaths became pants as she moved, striving to give herself over to the pleasure.

Meg pulled at her dress and I helped her out of it. My eyes drank in the sight of her. Her perfect curves, the light pink of her nipples, the luscious width of her hips. I would enjoy getting lost in this woman.

She held my face in her hands and her grin was full of promise. "Would my wolf care to hunt?"

My heart stuttered and my breath caught. My wolf. Now that she'd said it, I wanted her to call me that for the rest of our lives.

"I love a chase," I growled, trapped between rampaging lust and overwhelming affection.

Meg rose and ran for the water, diving in. Her shape sped toward the waterfall. Damn, she was fast. You'd have thought the woman was part selkie.

Her head broke the surface, but she dove back under and disappeared from view. My fingers fumbled with the clasp on my tartan, but I got it free and dropped it to the ground, diving in after her. The cold water rushed over me. I was a far less accomplished swimmer than she was, so by the time I made it to the waterfall, she was nowhere to be seen.

Her energy pulsed nearby, and I noticed an underwater tunnel. I took in a gasp of air and dove, swimming briskly through the narrow passage until it widened and I saw light overhead. As I broke the surface of the water, I realized the light was coming from a hole in the rocky ceiling, illuminating it just enough to see a small chamber, and ahead of me, a rough hewn set of stairs leading upward into the dark.

Meg was still somewhere ahead, so I forged on, cursing the water for dimming her scent. The steps were crumbling away. Whatever this place had been, no one had passed through here in ages. There was much more light ahead and I stepped out into a beautiful scene. Most of the rock ceiling had tumbled into the pool beneath it, and the interior teemed with ferns and other bright-green plant life.

There were at least five separate water sources coming in from the rocky walls, making many small waterfalls that fed the pool in the middle, which ultimately supplied the large waterfall that spilled into the cove below.

A soft noise from behind the fall on the far side of the space captured my attention, and I dove into the water, heading for it. When I broke the surface again, Meg was waiting for me, lying back on a flat stretch of rock bathed in sunlight that caught the waterfall and framed her in a million facets of color.

When my eyes snared hers, that animalistic hunger surged within me. The prey was mine. Her gaze scorched over me, and she grinned wickedly as she spread her knees wide. I reached forward and grasped her ankles, surprising her as I slid her to me on the slick rock, pulling her over the edge just enough to position her where I wanted her.

Her scent was something to luxuriate in as I moved between her thighs. I placed kisses and nips along her skin, teasing toward her apex. She squirmed in anticipation, her fingers wrapping in my hair as soon as I was within reach.

I chuckled and the burst of air against her wet pussy make her back arch. I ran my tongue between her slick folds and her breath hitched, fingers curling and thighs tightening around me. My tongue circled her clit and laved it with soft strokes before traveling lower and dipping into her soaked entrance.

She tasted sweet, and I licked my way back up to her nub, working it until her moans became gasps. She arched as I moved two fingers into her channel and pumped in and out of her while I kept my focus on her sensitive clit. She tensed and I increased my ministrations. With a final flick of my tongue, she came, her pussy clenching around my fingers.

I didn't let up until she came down, shaking as she collapsed back onto the stone. She tugged at my hair and I lifted myself out of the water as she pulled me into a kiss, tasting herself on me.

I startled as I looked into her eyes, swirling with a rainbow of iridescent colors. Meg noticed my shock and the haze of satisfaction quickly sharpened.

"What is it?"

"Your eyes. They're—"

I moved aside so Meg could see for herself. She leaned over the edge of the pool and stared at her reflection. "What in Tartarus's name?"

Chapter Twenty-Two

Meg

"Should we be worried about this?" I asked Gareth.

"This must be something else with the bonding."

"Am I going to shoot lasers out of my eyeballs?"

His eyes narrowed in confusion. "Lasers?"

I shook my head. "Sorry. Not sure how to explain that one."

"If anything, there's more to your own magick that we're about to find out."

"But—"

"Lass, if you don't take advantage of me this instant, I'm going to be very upset with you." His mouth twitched as he tried to hide a smile. "It'll be alright."

I reached out and traced the scars and tattoos on his chest with my fingertips and let myself sink into my power. I could feel him more acutely than I had before. Every sensation in my own body doubled as it was mirrored in his.

Moving away from the edge of the pool, I motioned him after me. He rose the rest of the way out of the water, revealing his impressive member at full attention. The need to taste him overpowered everything else.

With a light shove on his shoulders he lay down and watched as I dipped my head and licked the tip of his cock. He sucked in a breath. I worked his shaft into my mouth, tongue swirling around the smooth skin as I took him deeper. I cradled his balls in my hand as I kept working toward the base of his cock, opening my throat and moaning as my lips slid down the rest of the way.

Gareth was resisting his urge to move. If his experience was anything like mine was, it was a wonder. His desire and pleasure coursed through me as if they were my own, combined with the ache between my legs as I anticipated this massive cock sliding inside my tight pussy.

I bobbed, licking my way back up his shaft, swirling my tongue around the head and diving back down again, picking up my pace as I adjusted to the size of him gliding in and out of my throat. Saliva coated his dick as I worked, groaning around him as he gave the smallest of thrusts. I caught his eye, and he knew what I wanted. The thrusts became stronger, driving him deeper still into my throat.

I paused over him about halfway from the base and he held the back of my head as he fucked my face, my tongue attempting to keep up with his movement. I reached down between my legs and fingered myself, only a few stokes needed before I achieved orgasm, my cries muffled around his cock. He tensed and grunted as he came, hips freezing on his final thrust as he emptied himself down my throat.

I moaned, satiated. We were panting almost in sync when I drew my mouth off his dick with a slight pop as it left my lips. But we weren't done yet.

Gareth was still hard and a lazy smile came over his face as he invited me to take my pleasure any way I wanted it. I climbed up his body to straddle his hips and hovered for a moment.

His hands wandered up and down my body as he waited, teasing the stiff buds of my nipples, running down my thighs and around to cup my ass and back up again. I couldn't get enough of the hunger in his gaze, a man lost in the desert and I was his oasis.

I reached down and dragged his tip through my wetness, the surge of heat that ran through me almost overwhelming as he growled, a low rumble that reverberated throughout my body. He was bigger than anything I'd taken in the past, so I eased my way down onto his cock.

My channel stretched around him, pushed to its maximum, and I cried out when he was wholly inside me. I was full in the best way possible. As I rode him, his huge hands settled on my hips as I rocked, small thrusts keeping in rhythm.

I sensed something just behind my navel, an electric-shock type of thrill. Gareth gasped and I knew he felt it too. The magick had tethered between us. I paused, unsure, but Gareth bucked his hips to encourage me to continue.

My pace quickened as I raised myself up higher and dropped back down, but it still wasn't enough. I wanted to be taken, hard.

Again Gareth knew, without my needing to say anything, exactly what I needed. We repositioned, and he moved behind me as I settled on hands and knees, gripping my hips and sliding back into me. His thrusts were fierce and I gasped, crying out for more.

His hand moved between my folds and massaged my nub. I was so close.

Gareth bucked, driving into me harder, and I fell to pieces, the pleasure overwhelming me as the echo chamber of our connectedness overtook me.

I pulled Gareth's hand from my pussy and brought it to my lips, sucking his fingers into my mouth. He groaned and rocked, his hips smacking against me, the sound ricocheting around the space, eclipsed only by our moans.

The tether between us tightened, and we both came, exploding with cries of ecstasy. His thrusts continued as wave after wave of bliss went on with no sign of ebbing until it was too much. Every nerve ending was on fire, and I succumbed to the haze, unable to do anything but lie there and ride it through. Gareth's teeth grazed the back of my shoulder and his mouth clamped down, but he didn't break the skin. His wolf fangs extended and pricked my skin as his movements slowed.

I reached my hand up and caressed his hair. "Do it," I whispered.

Gareth bit down and broke the skin with one final thrust home. The magick coalesced around us and for an instant I couldn't breathe. Finally, the sensation faded, and I collapsed, exhausted. New power surged through me, utterly foreign. Gareth groaned and pulled me after him as he lay on his side, still inside me, this strange power flowing between us.

"Can you feel that?" I asked him.

His arms tightened around me, and he buried his face in the crook of my neck. "Aye. I've never known anything like it."

I hummed in pure satisfaction, but the hum turned into a low howl.

Gareth inhaled sharply. "Did you just—?"

We separated and sat up.

"Give me your hand," said Gareth excitedly, holding his hand up with the palm facing me. I pushed my hand against his and a tingling spread through my fingers and down toward my wrist. Claws erupted from Gareth's fingertips and my body reacted by matching his. There was no pain as my bones elongated and reshaped into clawed points. Gareth went even further with his transformation, and thick, black hair sprouted from his skin, the pads thickening on his palms.

A stronger surge of magick rose within me and soft, silver fur covered my hand. The tender pads rasped against his calloused ones.

Gareth lowered his hand. "Do you sense how the magick is different? How it works with your body to shift?"

"I think so." I focused on my hand and reversed the flow of energy, watching in amazement as it shifted back to normal.

Gareth got a glint in his eye of pure joy and stood, offering me his hand. "Let's go. We can run together."

"Try to keep up," I said, diving into the water.

When we surfaced in the pool and climbed to shore, I tapped into that strange magick.

"Wait!" Gareth barked.

I froze, looking around me. He crossed in front of me, eyes staring hard into every shadow, nostrils flaring, scenting for danger.

Then I noticed what had him on edge. Everything had gone silent and there was an eeriness to it that spoke to more than just human raiders lying in wait.

"It's Bel," I croaked. "He's figured it out. He's coming."

"Can you transport us?" Gareth's fingers laced through mine, his eyes still scanning for trouble.

We were both acutely aware of what Bel was capable of, and yet Gareth was ready to launch at him without hesitation.

"Yes." My resolve hardened, and I grabbed my dress before booking it back to camp, Gareth close on my heels.

A hum whined through the silence, and I could feel time wavering as the seams split, Bel forcing his way through. We dressed and gathered anything that would be useful for the journey.

I picked one of the remaining Six at random and pulled Gareth to me, wrapping my arms around him. "Whatever happens, I'm glad I found you."

Gareth smiled and leaned down for a kiss. I drew time around us and let it carry us away, toward destiny or death.

Only time would tell.

Coming Soon

The Primordial Embers Series Continues...
Look for a new release EVERY MONTH, six novellas in total!
Look for Book 2 in the series dropping July 30th, 2024

The Death's Left Hand Series:
Death's Left Hand Book 3 – October 8th, 2024
Death's Left Hand Book 4 – November 12th, 2024

Visit gwydionroyce.com or follow @gwydionroyce on insta-
gram and facebook for the latest updates!